Beach Trip

Laughs, Lies, and a Dash of Divine

JANE JENKINS HERLONG

Beach trip by Jane Jenkins Herlong
Published by Sweet Tea Publishing

ISBN: 978-1-965649-20-6
Copyright © 2026 by Jane Jenkins Herlong
Cover design by Hannah Linder Designs, hannahlinderdesigns.com
Interior design by atritex.com

Available in print from your local bookstore, online, or from the publisher.

For more information on this book and the author visit: janeherlong.com

All rights reserved. Non-commercial interests may reproduce portions of this book without the express written permission, provided the text does not exceed 500 words. When reproducing text from this book, include the following credit line: "*Beach Trip* by Jane Jenkins Herlong."

Commercial interests: No part of this publication may be reproduced in any form, stored in a retrieval system, or transmitted in any form by any means—electronic, photocopy, recording, or otherwise—without prior written permission of the publisher, except as provided by the United States of America copyright law.

This is a work of fiction. Names, characters, and incidents are all products of the author's imagination or are used for fictional purposes. Any mentioned brand names, places, and trade marks remain the property of their respective owners, bear no association with the author or the publisher, and are used for fictional purposes only.

Library of Congress Cataloging-in-Publication Data
Author's Herlong, Jane Jenkins
Beach Trip / Jane Jenkins Herlong 1st ed.

Printed in the United States of America

Author's Note

April 3, 2022, was supposed to be a celebration—my birthday.

Instead, it became a blur of fluorescent lights and hospital hallways. Thomas and I had been in three emergency rooms at three hospitals, all within a few days. He'd been hanging upside down on his inversion table when a searing pain slammed into his head—sudden, sharp, and far worse than any headache.

The good news? No serious damage.

The bad news? I had to say, for what felt like the hundredth time, "Thomas, you are not Batman. And you are definitely not twelve. Please stop hanging upside down on that thing."

Then came the call.

"Jane … Mary died in her sleep."

The air went still. My heart dropped straight to the soles of my feet.

Mary, my dear friend and beach buddy of over forty years, was suddenly gone.

No time to cry. No space to process.

Not then.

But maybe now—four years later.

Mary Holmes Johnston. Every page holds a piece of her—her joy, her grace, her quiet strength, and the wisdom she generously shared.

I'm writing this story because I miss Mary, plain and simple. What started as stories turned into something more: a love letter made of laughter, heartache, forgiveness, and the kind of friendship that doesn't fade, even after goodbye.

Yes, some parts are exaggerated, but only because I wanted Mary's beautiful qualities to shine a little brighter, her wisdom to ring a little louder, and her joy to linger a little longer. That's the gift of humor; it lets us hold on to what matters, even when life tries to take it away.

At its heart, this is the story of a beach trip shared by five girlfriends who met in college. And yes, it's a love story, but not the romantic kind. It's a heart-connection that shows up, holds space, and never leaves. But beneath the chaos, there is something deeply real.

It's messy. It's funny. It's tender.

And like any good girls' trip, it became exactly what they didn't know they needed.

You won't meet the girls all at once, but little by little, they'll unfold like a well-worn beach towel. One misplaces more than her sunglasses these days. Another moves through the world with a quiet bravery, holding tightly to moments others take for granted. One still sets an extra place at the table. Another tiptoes through a marriage that no longer feels like home. And then there's the preacher's wife—sassy, sanctified, and unpredictable enough to keep the rest of them from falling apart.

This is more than a girls' trip. It's a reckoning wrapped in laughter, carried on ocean breezes. So as you read, think about your own beach trips—the sunburns and laughs, yes—but also the difficult truths that rise up when the tide pulls everything else away.

Because this weekend? It's not just about the memories. It's about the mending.

Jane Jenkins Herlong

Beach Trip

Laughs, Lies, and a Dash of Divine

Chapter One

Mary Jo eased her Bronco past the old convenience store off Highway 501, its rusted Sinclair dinosaur sign swaying in the wind. Funny ... once the green logo gleamed like new. She pictured the Second Floor Girls piled into her Camaro, barefoot and sunburned, laughing too loud as they dashed inside for cheap beer like it was a rite of passage.

That first beach trip—Lord, they'd worn that story out for thirty years. And it never got old.

The memory played in her mind like an eight-track stuck on repeat. The flashing blue lights, the officer leaning into the window.

"You drinkin'?" he asked.

And Bertie, quick as lightning, "You buyin'?"

Somehow, they got off with a warning—bolder, luckier, sure the good times would never end.

Mary Jo knuckled her eye, clearing her vision. Forever had ended too soon. Last year's trip blurred beneath a cloud of grief. Charles was gone. A heart attack. No warning. No time. Her world spun off its axis. More than once, she had stopped at green lights, plowed through red ones. Couldn't focus. Couldn't breathe. The weight of loss pressed down on everything.

Her counselor had said, "One day you'll laugh through the tears." And eventually, she would—at the vet's office of all places. After dropping off her oversized German Shepherd to be neutered, the vet called her back into the room.

"Mary Jo, I can't charge you for this. This dog's already been fixed."

She squinted at the poor thing and deadpanned, "Well, mind double-checkin'? He sure doesn't act like it."

That was the first time laughter truly returned. Like Charles, Beau still had a spark in his step. Humor hadn't left her, just taken the long way home.

The day before leaving for their annual beach trip, Mary Jo had held up her swimsuit and chuckled. What used to be a bikini was now a full-on cover-up. Lands' End, page 62. Mercy, she used to shop on page 15. She gave her backside a playful pinch and shook her head. *If the Lord wanted me to have a Brazilian booty, He'd have mailed a coupon for a Delta voucher.*

But humor wasn't the only thing she had packed. Before zipping her suitcase, she walked into the dining room and looked at Charles' portrait. Silent words rose from her soul.

Charles ... I've held on to you for so long. Through vows, through memories, through silence. But Jackie—one of my Second Floor Girls, you know the one—she needs me. Not the half-alive version I've been. The full Mary Jo. The one who laughs, who lifts, who walks beside her. She needs that Mary Jo. Maybe even all the way to the end.

She steadied herself with a chair. I don't want to let you go, my dear Charles. But maybe ... I need to let you let me go.

Because that's what the Second Floor Girls—or SFG as they called themselves—did. Held space for each other, one friend at a time. They stayed close when the world went quiet.

Soft as sea foam. Steady as grace.

This year, though, Mary Jo wasn't sure grace and laughter would be enough. Jackie hadn't said much since the diagnosis. Not about her future. Not about anything.

So Mary Jo had slipped something extra into her suitcase— their senior yearbook. Just in case Jackie needed to see the words they once wrote to each other. Words Mary Jo couldn't yet say out loud.

Aiming the Bronco toward the exit ramp, she gripped the wheel tighter and whispered into the hum of the highway, "This year ... we make space in our place for wounds to heal."

Chapter Two

Vivian fluffed the decorative pillow into place and delivered a clean karate chop right down the middle. Her momma would have been proud. The house stood ready. The richness of fresh varnish rode in with the salt wind, both clinging to back-porch screens that seemed to catch the fullness of life lived at the edge of the land.

She stood still on the bedroom veranda, the boards warm beneath her feet, her gaze dropping to the street below. Golf carts passed in slow rhythm, each driver stealing a glance at the house that had turned heads all winter. The shutters, the symmetry, the confidence in its frame … it was all there, standing firm.

She was determined to do the same.

Vivian moved to the front porch, the land breeze brushing the hem of her Lilly Pulitzer dress. For once, the skittering of drafts working their way in from the back porch, through the house and out, brought no thrill. The polished floors, the monogrammed linens, the hush of envy in a neighbor's throat. None of it reached her the way it used to.

A car door thudded shut next door. Its jarring sound sent a tremor through her soul. A warning? No, simply renters checking in.

Concern for Arthur filled her mind. Columbia. His work at the hospital. His signature strut through tiled corridors. Women who waited months to sit across from him in soft gowns and under fluorescent light and have him confirm, after an all-too-invasive examination, that they were still whole and healthy, able to bear children.

His name still opened doors. His work kept hers closed.

He hadn't come to the beach in months. Always working. Always a conference. Always a reason.

She filed that thought into a place she'd examine later. After a drink, maybe. Or several.

This weekend wasn't for appearances. It wasn't for Arthur. It was for Jackie.

Vivian had always been the steady one—the one who swept past grief and looked good doing it. But this weekend wasn't about bouncing back. It was about standing still, shoulder to shoulder, when standing was all you could manage.

And that made everything feel thin around the edges. One raw comment, one slurred, off-handed jest too many and the group might scatter, never to return.

The phone rang. Again.

She dropped into the rocking chair, the slats pressing against her spine, and answered. Her fingers tapped the armrest to the slow beat of an old Tams tune, "Be Young, Be Foolish, Be Happy," that still lived in muscle memory.

"Someone'll be there," she said. "Mary Jo's picking you up." She softened her tone, let it stretch with sugar.

"Mary … Jo?" The name hung there. Bertie's voice carried no anchor.

"That's right," Vivian said.

"Oh. Okay then."

Vivian paused. "We'll see you soon." She ended the call and tapped the wood again. "Don't let love slip away," she sang under her breath.

She stared at the horizon but didn't see it.

Arthur had once danced with her to that song. Back before his phone rang all night and he stopped looking at her when she spoke.

She closed the memory without mourning it.

Beach Week used to be her favorite stretch of the year. Now it came with pill bottles in makeup bags and calls from Bertie asking the same question twice.

Still, she cherished the time. How many more memories could the SFG make? In the same way stains from rusty nails stretched down porch railings, the girls were aging—and not always in attractive ways.

Bertie's stories fell apart now. Eager to say more, too often her memory betrayed her. But if anyone could gather the loose threads of the past and lay them gently back into place, it was Mary Jo. With Mary Jo, tomorrow had the possibility of your best day ever.

Chapter Three

Mary Jo remembered the heat as she stood in line outside Columbia Women's College on registration day. Her feet ached inside cheap white sandals not built for waiting. She remembered the girl beside her with a voice full of sass and polyester misery. Vivian. That day began their many years as friends.

They'd both come from small towns that clung to tradition like old wallpaper. Both spoke fluent sarcasm. Both rolled their eyes in unison when handed identical dorm keys. They moved in as strangers and by midnight had already confessed the best and worst of everything.

They majored in education and minored in Kappa Alpha frat boys, electives they took more than once.

They raced the hands of the clock and the rulebook—top down, hair wild, mascara weeping from laughter. Mary Jo's Camaro roared through downtown Columbia in the dark, while Vivian clutched the dashboard and the curfew loomed like a badge they never planned to earn.

The housemother waited by the door, robe cinched tight, jaw tighter. But she always stepped aside. Just in time.

Every spring, Old South Weekend rolled in hot and loud. That year, Mary Jo's date arrived with his Confederate uniform buttoned wrong, while Vivian's date staggered through the Hilton's ballroom, half-blind from nickel beer at Crazy Zack's.

The Hilton's ballroom filled with the scent of cheap beer and borrowed valor. The boys mumbled secession speeches between gulps from briefcase bars.

They hovered near the punch bowl with a hand-lettered warning—*Purple Jesus Punch Freshman Girls Only*—and drank anyway.

Whispers of rebellion followed them across the room. One girl—no one agrees who—suggested the ultimate Southern mutiny: lure the boys out of their uniforms "for the Cause." The boys, eager and unsteady, obliged.

Stripped and stumbling, their pride as exposed as the rest of them, they never noticed the girls had slipped over the rise in full retreat.

Mary Jo and Vivian crammed into Vivian's green Pinto, air thick with Aqua Net and Boone's Farm. Vivian could barely see the road. Her hoop skirt had ballooned so high it covered the steering wheel.

By second semester of their junior year, both had rings on their fingers and wedding plans penciled into their diaries. The entire second floor didn't wait long before they pounced. They swarmed in without warning, snatching books from laps amidst protests of betrayal. But soon, squeals and laughter swallowed the hurt feelings.

In celebration, they paraded across the lawn, veils of toilet paper billowing behind them. And in front of the red-brick mansion where it all began, they were tackled by a mob of classmates still in curlers.

They landed in the fountain with a splash that silenced the campus for a beat, then popped the peace open with shrieks, cheers, and a curler-strewn war cry.

Not long after graduation, they stood shoulder to shoulder in lace and laughter, already rehearsing for the day they'd trade roles as maid of honor. Those pastel dresses still hung on padded hangers, just above the Peau De Soie heels they vowed never to wear again—but couldn't bring themselves to toss.

Within a few short years, bassinets and baby showers took center stage—Vivian with Georgia, Mary Jo with Virginia. The girls arrived only weeks apart, born into friendship.

After the weddings and the baby showers came the rituals.

Wednesday mornings at nine. Morning Coffee Chat.

Nothing intruded upon that sacred hour. Not husbands, not headlines, not hailstorms.

They talked about everything: SFG updates, cholesterol numbers, who was dating whom, what the husbands had done or hadn't.

And then Charles died.

The rhythm fractured. His absence moved into the house like mold—creeping into closets, coating silence in every room.

The Second Floor Girls wrapped her in a kind of love she hadn't known she needed: soft, steady, ever-present.

But Vivian came when the casseroles stopped.

She didn't call first. She didn't ask what Mary Jo needed. She just appeared, every Sunday that hollowed into ache.

Sometimes with a sack of groceries—the receipt folded, her lipstick kiss pressed faintly into the paper. Sometimes with a bouquet wrapped in butcher paper and tape, still wet from the flower market. Sometimes with nothing but the hush of her car door, the rhythm of her heels on brick, and the creak of the storm door before she stepped through.

She never filled the silence with talk. She filled it with her presence.

Mary Jo never forgot those moments, how Vivian eased into the nearest chair, pulled it close, and said with everything except words: *You don't have to do this alone.*

Mary Jo no longer cared to pretend. Grief had hollowed her out long enough. She missed the girl who tore down Main Street in a Camaro. She missed her youth, her past, and if not careful, soon her future.

Now, all these years later, she stood ready in cushioned white sandals to find that girl again.

Chapter Four

Vivian memorized the way Mary Jo stood at Charles' funeral: chin high, shoulders squared, holding steady while the rest of her life cracked beneath her heels. Vivian didn't know why she watched so closely that day. Only that something in her had filed it away, the way you do when you sense a storm long before the clouds roll in.

After Mary Jo became a widow, the girls circled her with casseroles, weekend check-ins, and enough laughter to keep her tethered.

But now, it was Jackie who needed them.

Vivian felt it in her chest … a low, quiet throb of fear she didn't want to name. Jackie's diagnosis had shifted the center of their circle. It wasn't grief creeping in this time; it was something colder, more precise. It had a name, a timeline, and no intention of waiting.

Vivian didn't know how to fix it. But she knew one thing: she had to keep the Second Floor Girls close. All of them. She'd hold this weekend together the best she could. If that meant pretending, so be it.

Still, the thought of Arthur's distance lingered, just beneath the surface where the truth likes to wait.

The crunch of tires on gravel rescued her. Mary Jo's Bronco pulled into the designated landing pad for luggage, casseroles, and Bertie. Vivian rushed down the steps.

"Well now," Mary Jo called, "when did you finish the landscaping, Viv? Last time I was here, you couldn't decide on a thing."

Vivian waved a hand toward the flower beds. "Oh, you know how all this hoo-ha works. If your neighbor's yard looks fabulous, it's practically your civic duty to copy it."

Mary Jo grinned. "Look at you, Viv! Have you dropped some pounds?"

Vivian slapped her arm gently. "Hush! You know just how to make a girl feel ten years younger." She stretched out her arms, the gold bracelet catching the light.

"Viv! Where on earth did you get that bracelet?"

"I was dyin' to tell you, Mary Jo. Arthur pulled one of his surprises. Told me to detour through Charleston on the way down and stop at Calhouns."

Mary Jo gasped. "Don't tell me. He got you the double gold chain with the diamonds? Hand engraved? Every woman at the Rock Hill Women's Club has been talkin' about that bracelet for weeks!"

Vivian smiled. "Suga, you can't put a price on love. Arthur said the double chains were us—twisted together. And the diamonds? One for every year since we met. Thirty, if you can believe it." She hesitated, running her thumb across the clasp.

"Is *priceless* ever on sale? My Charles would never have bought it full price. He was more practical than poetic. Steady, yes, but the only thing he ever surprised me with was a new air filter."

Vivian caught the flicker of humor in her voice. Small, but real.

They wrapped each other in a hug, warm and familiar. But a glance toward the Bronco pulled them back. Bertie sat still in the front seat, hands folded neatly in her lap, watching with that soft, faraway look.

"Oh, Lord," Mary Jo whispered. "She's just sittin' there."

Arms looped around each other's waist, they stood in quiet stillness.

"It's worse than I thought," Mary Jo said. "On the way here, she kept askin' what we were doin' for Spring Break. Thought we were headed to Ocean Drive."

Vivian didn't flinch. "Then Spring Break it is. If that's where Bertie's mind is, we'll meet her there—by the grace of God." She stepped to the car, opened the door, and smiled. "Come on, girlfriend."

Bertie looked around, confused but calm. "Viv, I don't remember this house at all. Should I?"

Vivian reached for her hand. "Suga, we just moved in. This is our very first SFG beach trip here. And you've got the best room in the house."

Bertie stepped carefully out, her smile uncertain.

Inside, Mary Jo dropped Bertie's suitcase by one of the guest rooms. "Let's get you settled."

Bertie unzipped the case, hesitated, then frowned. "These are all dirty. I thought I packed for the beach, but … this is laundry." She held up a wrinkled blouse smudged with something that might've been lipstick or jelly—or both. "When did I even wear this?"

Vivian gave a soft laugh, already opening a nearby drawer. "Well, lucky for you, the SFG wardrobe is open for business. You'll be our beach babe model."

Mary Jo knelt beside the bag, her voice gentle. "Don't worry, Bert. We'll find you something fabulous until we can get to a store."

Bertie gave a sheepish smile. "Y'all always did dress better than me anyway."

The bags had barely touched the floor when the phone rang. Mary Jo glanced at her screen. John, Bertie's husband. Without a word, she handed Bertie the phone.

"Hey, honey! Yes, we're here. I thought we were headed to Ocean Drive, but we pulled into Viv's house instead. Isn't that silly?" She laughed, light and carefree. "It's just beautiful, and I'm having the best time …"

Mary Jo stepped onto the porch and quietly shut the door.

Vivian noticed her wiping the corner of her eye. "What's wrong? Is Bertie okay?"

Mary Jo gave a soft smile. "That sweet John. He just called to check in with Bertie. And to let me know she took the wrong suitcase. The one he packed for her is still by the door in their bedroom."

"You think she's okay?"

Mary Jo paused, keeping her voice low. "She's better than okay. Before we left, I asked John if he had a plan … you know, for when things get worse. I mentioned Wildwood Commons."

A chill crawled up Vivian's spine. She nodded slowly. "And?"

"He said no."

"No?"

Mary Jo looked at her, eyes glassy but steady. "Did you know he was offered the CEO job at Meta Life?"

Vivian shook her head. "Lawd, have mercy."

"They told him, 'Someday, she won't know you.'" Mary Jo's breath caught. "And John said, 'Yes … but I'll always know her.'"

Vivian didn't speak. Couldn't. The weight of those words sank deep … into her chest, into the quiet. She reached out and touched Mary Jo's arm.

Chapter Five

Mary Jo stood at the railing, eyes tracking the surf as it tumbled in, then slid back out—a rhythm she usually found comforting. Not today.

Bertie.

The name still carried weight back home in Edgefield County. She had heard it spoken with pride and fear in equal measure. Even now, folks couldn't bring up the old courthouse without mentioning Bertie's family name.

And at Columbia Women's College? Bertie had been a legend. Chair of the Judicial Council, sharp as a gavel, never raised her voice—and didn't need to. Girls used to hold their breath when those pink slips landed in mail slots.

"That's the Honorable Beatrice Mims Rainsford," they said. "Don't sass her, don't cross her, and for heaven's sake, don't be late."

Mary Jo had watched her rise all the way from campus to the Capitol. She remembered the day Bertie got the call from Senator Thurmond himself. They all knew it was coming. Tulane Law. The D.C. Circuit. Bertie didn't chase dreams. She subpoenaed them.

The Supreme Court whispers had been real. At least, until that law school speech.

Mary Jo hadn't been there in person, but she'd heard from a friend who was.

"She started strong," the woman said. "Then the words just … stopped. Like she'd stepped out of her own body."

No press release. No announcement. But everyone knew. Mary Jo had known too. The forgetting had begun.

That was the thing about Alzheimer's. It didn't take everything at once; it took it in fragments. And Bertie? She'd always given herself to everything. Now the world was taking her back, piece by piece.

Mary Jo felt the familiar twist in her chest.

Vivian joined her at the railing. "You know, Mary Jo," she said quietly, "I haven't said this to anyone else."

Mary Jo turned toward her, one brow slightly raised.

"With everything going on with Bertie, with Jackie, I catch myself feeling ... off. Not sad. Something else."

"I'd say I know the feeling, but with Charles, mine was nothing like that."

"I've got Arthur. He spoils me rotten. We've got Georgia, this house, friends, good health. Everything seems so perfect. And still ..." Vivian's voice trailed off. "There's this knot in my chest that won't let go."

Mary Jo's hand reached for hers, warm and steady. "Sixth sense."

"Exactly."

The door creaked before Bertie stepped through.

"What are you girls whisperin' about?" she asked, her smile turned up a touch too high.

"Oh, we didn't want to interrupt your call with John," Vivian offered gently.

Bertie narrowed her eyes. "Did he call me?"

Mary Jo was quick. "Doesn't matter one bit, sweetie."

"Hey, here's an idea," Vivian said. "Let's take a ride in the golf cart before the other two show up."

The golf cart bumped over a cracked seashell driveway, tires crunching through a patch of sand that had blown in overnight. A seagull swooped low over the marsh to their left, shrieking its protest at the midday heat.

Mary Jo's phone buzzed in her lap. She glanced at the screen. "Accountant."

Vivian raised a brow and looked over her sunglasses. "Uh-oh."

Nudging her sunhat into place, Bertie asked from the back seat, "Out of money?"

"No idea." Mary Jo tapped to answer and turned slightly away. "But hearing from an accountant unannounced is never good." Her voice lowered to a private register.

Vivian exchanged a glance with Bertie, then reached into the top of a small cooler wedged between her legs. "Bertie, ready for your toddy?"

"As long as it's wet, chilled, and not Boone's Farm—yes."

Vivian pulled out the bottle. "It's Boone's Farm."

"Oh, why not?" Bertie held out her plastic tumbler. "It's beach time."

Vivian twisted the cork with a flourish and poured a splash. "A rare vintage. I think you'll like it."

Bertie sipped and gave a look of surprise. "No way this is the same wine we drank in college."

"Arthur has become something of a wine snob." Vivian filled her cup. "Or rather, I should say, he's a snob who fancies himself as a wine expert."

Mary Jo ended her call and, slipping her phone back into her bag, asked, "We drinking?"

Bertie raised her glass. "To old times and new memories."

Vivian handed Mary Jo a Clemson tumbler half-filled with rosé. "You broke?"

Mary Jo shrugged. "He didn't actually say. Something about Charles' old accounts. But if I am broke ..."

They clinked their tumblers and said in unison, "Go out in style!"

Rolling on, the cart continued along the narrow cart path, its tires whirring beneath their chatter.

"See that big contemporary house on the inlet? That's Paulie and Nancy's place.

They're from the Jersey Shore.

Vivian gripped the steering wheel of the golf cart, eyes on the path, voice dropping to a whisper.

"Nancy's been married three times."

Mary Jo shook her head.

Vivian leaned in, smirking. "The first two were useless. Never lifted a finger to help her. So when they died, she had them both cremated. Kept them on her mantel—separate urns—just staring at her every day."

Mary Jo blinked. "And?"

Vivian nodded, enjoying every word. "One morning, she marched to the funeral home, bought a jumbo urn, dumped them both in together, gave it a good shake and said, 'Y'all made life miserable—now you can spend eternity together. Rest in peace. I'm finally gonna live in it.'"

Mary Jo slapped her knee. "You're kidding."

Vivian's smile turned wicked. "Then she poured the ashes into an hourglass."

Bertie blinked. "Why an hourglass?"

Vivian leaned back, satisfied. "Because those two may have been useless in life but they've become useful in death. Their ashes time her poached egg every morning."

Bertie frowned. "But ... doesn't that get ash in the eggs?"

Mary Jo let out an unexpected laugh. "Only if *Nancy's* cracked, honey—not the hourglass."

"Lawd," Vivian said, "I thought we had stories. Arthur met Paulie on the golf course and said he was hilarious. We went out to dinner with them one night, and I'm not kiddin', they talked nonstop about absolutely nothing. Every other sentence was loaded with F-bombs. It was like a live-action episode of *The Sopranos*. I kept hearing, 'You guys, you guys …' and I'm sitting there thinking, *It's y'all, suga. You're in the South now.*

"Arthur swears Paulie's got mob ties," Vivian continued. "I told him if he disappears after their next golf game, I'm not asking questions. I'm just cashing in the life insurance."

Mary Jo sighed. "Another Yankee reached the Promised Land."

"But I'll tell you what," Vivian added. "Everybody in this neighborhood loves them. They're our Southern-Fried Yankees. Kiss you on the cheek but still honk at you in traffic."

Passing a sleek glass house next, all steel angles and smudged windows, Vivian said, "Lana Crenshaw lives there now."

"Lana who?" asked Bertie.

"She did that TED Talk on intention and bread-making. Been there once. Home smells like yeast and regret. Previous owners moved back to Charlotte after their youngest got into UNC. Couldn't handle the humidity. She used to walk their schnauzer in a baby stroller. That dog wore sunglasses. Would not shut up."

"Dogs are like that," said Mary Jo.

"I meant Lana," Vivian replied.

Sounding uncertain, Bertie asked, "Did I ever meet her?"

Mary Jo reached back and gently patted her knee. "Once or twice."

"Remind me."

"You waved from this cart and told her that dog had better fashion sense than most pageant moms. Lana laughed so hard she rolled the stroller into a sprinkler head."

Bertie smiled. "Sounds like something I'd say or do."

Vivian steered around a curve, waving at a man pressure-washing his pontoon boat. "The Cunninghams' old place. Guy that owns it now is retired NYPD. His wife's allergic to shrimp."

"I used to be allergic to bananas," Bertie added. "Made my throat itch."

"I remember that," said Mary Jo. "You did this thing with your tongue that made it look like you were about to throw up."

"I never knew that," Vivian said. "All those times I served banana pudding you never said anything."

"I grew out of it, I guess. If I did, I can't remember when."

The cart bounced over a speed bump, and Bertie raised her tumbler in a mock toast. "To new neighbors and forgotten allergies!"

"And keeping it breezy and boozy," Mary Jo chimed in.

They slowed near the marsh boardwalk, sunlight shimmering across the pluff mud and marsh grass. A salt breeze danced over them, lifting Vivian's bangs as the cart rolled past a stretch of sea oats bending in the breeze, golden tips catching the sun. The hush between them carried a sacred silence, as if the three knew not to fill it too quickly.

Mary Jo broke the quiet, her voice low and deliberate. "I was taught that grief comes in tidy little stages: denial, anger, bargaining, depression, acceptance. Now I think it just circles back around, like a dog looking for a place to lie down. Restless, familiar, and never quite finished."

Vivian gave a soft laugh, dry and knowing. "Grief doesn't stage anything. It simply shows up uninvited and unannounced. It eats all your snacks, then has the nerve to stay for dessert."

Mary Jo smiled. "Charles would've loved that line. He always said you had a way of making hard things land soft."

Vivian shifted in her seat, brushing a windblown strand from her cheek. Her voice dropped, thoughtful. "Every time I get to the beach, it's like something lifts. And then I realize why and feel a little guilty. I haven't called Arthur. Or Georgia. Hate to say it, but with both, I'm always one wrong word away from finding myself in the middle of an argument that means nothing except I'm sad and mad when it's over. I tell myself hearing their voices helps keep me centered, and that's true. But Lord knows, sometimes ... sometimes I wonder if Arthur gives a rip if I call or not. On the phone, he always sounds like I'm bothering him."

Mary Jo looked over. "Just be glad you've got a husband to call."

At the thought of Mary Jo walking into her house alone—with no one asking about her trip or how much she spent—Vivian said, "I'm sorry. I shouldn't have brought it up."

"It's okay. I'm fine. Like I said, my old dog Grief keeps circling, looking for my lap to crawl up in. But I mean it, Viv. I hope you know how lucky you are. Not to mention how lucky Virginia is. Arthur has been like a father-figure to her since Charles' heart attack. He has been there for her when she needed something fixed."

Vivian reached across the cart and took Mary Jo's hand, her grip warm, deliberate. "I do. And I appreciate you." Glancing over her shoulder, she added, "You too, Bertie."

She pressed the pedal gently as the cart hummed forward through the warm South Carolina air, leaving behind tire tracks, wine buzz, and just enough love to hold back the tide.

"And Lori Anne. And Jackie."

"And Arthur," Mary Jo added.

"You're right. I should call Arthur and tell him what a wonderful time I'm having. Maybe if I focused less on what he does wrong and more on the fact that he still loves me ..." She lifted her wrists, showing off the bracelet.

"Oh my gosh," Bertie interrupted. "I need to call John and tell him I'm here."

Vivian shot Mary Jo a look. A warning. A silent confession that this may be the last beach trip for the five. The next time there may only be four ... or three ... or none.

Chapter Six

Mary Jo traced the rim of her glass, condensation slick against her finger. Outside, the incoming tide whispered with rhythmic exhalations, nature's calming voice that Mary Jo so very much loved. Overhead, the ceiling fan clicked a quiet rhythm, slicing warm air that clung to their skin like memory.

Vivian sat across from her, fingers draped on the stem of her wine glass, eyes scanning the room as though seeing her guests in a new light and with a clarity that revealed every wrinkle and cosmetic scar.

"Remind me," Bertie said. "Whose house is this?"

Mary Jo caught Vivian's glance of shock before her focus returned to Bertie.

"Arthur built it for me, suga."

Mary Jo gave Vivian the faintest nod, as if warning her to play along.

"Oh." Bertie looked down at her tea. "That's right. I feel so stupid sometimes."

"That's me all the time," Mary Jo said. "I can't tell you how many times I've walked into my kitchen and forgotten why."

Vivian reached across and took Bertie's hand. "You remembered the important part. You came."

Bertie gave a soft smile and turned her gaze back toward the sea.

Mary Jo shifted in her chair, nudging the moment forward. "It is a beautiful home, Viv. Even though we talked about moving for years and even engaged a realtor once, I'm still in our little dream house, that brick ranch. Charles never wanted more than one level and a place to tinker. Now, having a main bedroom on the first floor is a smart move since I'm not getting any younger. His man cave's still packed to the rafters with gear from boats he sold years ago. I suppose one day, if it comes to that, a nurse or caregiver could sleep there."

Vivian leaned back, her glass dangling from two fingers. "Mary Jo, tell me you're not still living like a librarian on a church salary. Charles left you with something, didn't he?"

"If he did, I don't know about it. The accountant Charles used handles all my finances. He sends everything to Virginia's office in Atlanta. You know that numbers turn my brain to soup. Only thing I've ever asked him was to let me know ahead of time if I'm about to go broke."

Vivian's lips lifted. "Well, it's good you have Virginia watching your money. That girl came into this world two steps ahead and hasn't slowed down since. She's a paralegal, but truth be told, she's practically running the whole law firm—and in Atlanta, no less. That's no small thing."

Mary Jo savored the compliment for a moment, then the old ache returned. The distance. The silence. The way Virginia never seemed to find time to call or text. A reminder of how close her only child had been to Charles.

Vivian, perhaps sensing where Mary Jo's head was going, leaned in, her tone softening. "All I'm saying is, quit clipping coupons. Buy something outrageous. Take a trip. Let your hair down and raise a little hell like you used to."

Bertie let out a short laugh. Mary Jo shook her head, then gave in, shoulders bouncing. Vivian followed, catching the unexpected humor of her comment. If anyone was far from hell, it was Mary Jo.

Their laughter built, rolling between them until footsteps struck the stairs, each one harder, faster, cutting through the sound.

"Lori Anne, is that you?" Viv asked.

Lori Anne pushed open the back-porch door, clothes bags hanging off arms, heels clicking. Voice full of gladness, she exclaimed, "Well, girls, I'm here! Have mercy, Viv! It took me ten whole minutes to get through the circle. Did this house get bigger? Land sakes, our church parsonage could fit inside your foyer."

Lori Anne had always been too much for polite company. Eyeshadow that sparkled like Christmas tinsel, ripped jeans tight as skin, a red top cut low, a matching bra she didn't mind showing, and stiletto heels that slapped the floor with every wobbling step.

Mary Jo eyed the shoes. "You're gonna break your neck walking up and down porch steps in those."

"I know." Lori Anne grinned. "But The Sassy Magnolia's truck rolled in, and these were on clearance. Add a little Charmin and, honey, you'll look downright charmin'!"

Mary Jo cackled. "Well, come on over and give us a hug before that toilet paper disintegrates."

She beamed at them. "Oh, y'all. I've been smilin' for days."

Vivian leaned toward Mary Jo, voice low. "Hard to tell. Botox froze most of her face."

"I heard that!"

Vivian grinned. "Suga, you best tell us how you feel—your face isn't saying a word."

Lori Anne waved her off. "Anyway, did I mention Sammie's new church? We moved to Hell Hole Swamp."

Vivian sputtered into her wine. "That's not a location, that's a warning."

"It's real! And y'all know the Lord has a sense of humor, 'cause He sent yours truly—Miss Hell Hole Swamp, 19 …" She coughed just in time to bury the year. "Anyway, as I was sayin', Miss Hell Hole Swamp is back. I told the deacons they weren't just gettin' a preacher, they were gettin' royalty. A modern-day Queen Esther, Southern style. I even brought my crown. Had it tucked right next to the deviled eggs in my quilted casserole carrier."

Mary Jo gave Lori Anne her full attention. "Do Lawd, what'd Sammie say?"

"He said I went overboard. I told him, 'Overboard? Honey, *I am* the boat.'"

Vivian took a sip so slow it might've been for show. "That man's been married to a full parade float for thirty years and only now figured it out?"

"Dear Lawd, I've got more luggage than should be legal. Will somebody grab that big suitcase out of my Lexus and my makeup bag?"

It took all four of them to lug her bags up the stairs—two canvas totes, a rolling hard case, and a leopard-print vanity bag that clanged with something glassy inside.

"Viv, I thought this place had an elevator."

"It's broken."

"Of course it is. Just when we need it most."

At the landing, Lori Anne stopped short, breath catching. "Heavens above! I left my Bible on the passenger seat, and I want to show you my Louis Vuitton Bible carrier."

"You're making that up," Bertie replied.

"I wouldn't lie about Louis!"

Vivian jerked her head toward her. "Wait a minute. Are you tellin' me Louis Vuitton's in the Bible business now?"

"Sort of. I got Sammie to burn the name into the leather with his little wood-burnin' pen. Don't look too close, though. He spelled it L-E-W-I-E."

Mary Jo caught herself smiling. Ridiculous, wonderful woman.

Most girls at CWC never knew what to make of Lori Anne. Too loud. Too shiny. Too much for the silver-spoon crowd. But the Second Floor Girls had seen through the rhinestones to the heartbeat beneath.

Mary Jo paused on the top step, one hand on the rail, letting the memory pull her back.

Not long after Lori Anne showed up at CWC, she went to First Baptist Church's Bible study. A handsome preacher, Rhett Younger, took the pulpit. Hair like honey and a voice that could crack stone. One Sunday night, Lori Anne marched straight to the altar, eyes shining, and gave her life to the Lord. She strutted down that church aisle like a beauty queen walking a pageant runway.

She'd told the SFG the next morning, with both hands in the air and joy spilling from every pore.

A week later, the rest of them had followed.

Yes, the message had stirred their souls, but the preacher's dimples hadn't hurt either.

Vivian said that altar call didn't feel holy; it felt like a stampede of hormones on steroids. She expected someone to throw a phone number into the offering plate.

That was only the beginning.

Lori Anne had become their dorm-floor oracle. If you were weeping over a breakup, failing chemistry, or needed to scream into a pillow, you went to Room 206. The red bandana tied to the doorknob meant she was in session. No appointments. Just knock, enter, and sit down with a Tab, a verse, and whatever country song was playing low from her cassette deck.

Even now, Mary Jo could hear Lori Anne's voice quoting Ruth one second and Reba the next. And always, always ready to pray.

Mary Jo reached for the leopard-print vanity bag. "Come on, Queen Esther. Let's get our Miss Hell Hole Swamp settled."

Lori Anne managed her widest grin. Her face might have been frozen, but her heart overflowed with gratitude.

Chapter Seven

At the text from Jackie that she was an hour out, the four women scattered to their rooms—unpacking, changing, checking mirrors to see what facial feature needed making up. Their first-night tradition held. No cooking, dinner out, and a dash of mischief—just enough to remind five CWC roomies who they used to be.

Mary Jo unzipped her overnight case and called through the open door, "Viv, you got an extra hair dryer? Mine's dead."

"You sure it's the dryer? Check the outlet. Might need to be reset."

"Done that already. Lamp works."

"Check the hall closet," Vivian called back from her bedroom. "Middle shelf, behind the beach towels."

From down the hall, Bertie called, "Y'all got a nail clipper?"

Mary Jo ducked into her bathroom, then into the hall. Rummaging through towels, she called, "Middle shelf?"

"Is it not there?" Viv answered.

"Oh, lower, got it." On her way back, she tossed nail clippers on Bertie's bed.

From the opposite room, Lori Anne asked, "Did you hear anything from Virginia?"

"Not a word. Three texts. Not even an emoji."

"Hey, check your phones," Vivian said. "There's a text from Jackie."

"Drying off," Bertie called back. "Just read it."

"My dear SFG, this trip won't be like the others. Too much has changed, but my heart's still strong. Emotionally, anyway. Please, no fussing over me. I'm still me, just with a different look."

Mary Jo lowered the volume on their Beach Trip playlist. "Damn imaging center. Four reschedules. She waited almost two months. Now it's Stage Four. Hope she sues them."

"What good would it do?" Viv asked. "She'll never live long enough to see any settlement money."

The AC clicked on, its hum intruding on the silence.

"Hey, MJ, you remember when we met Jackie?"

"Lawd, yes." Mary Jo caught the opening notes of the next song and bumped up the volume. "We thought we'd hit the jackpot. Four of us in the biggest corner dorm room on campus. Space for a couch even. We hadn't planned on a fifth."

"But then," Bertie said quietly, "there she was—alone on the back bleachers, the only Black girl in the CWC gym."

"She didn't flinch," said Lori Anne.

"But you did, Bertie," said Viv.

"Couldn't help it. My upbringing."

"And yet, somehow, that space built for four became the perfect fit for five," Mary Jo said. "She changed everything."

Vivian joined Mary Jo in the hallway.

With a brush in one hand and mascara in the other, she asked, "Y'all remember that scholarship she set up?"

"Three hundred students." Lori Anne leaned against the doorframe of her bedroom. "All because Jackie thought everyone should have a shot at college."

"First one of us to get a job too," Mary Jo added. "Drove herself to D.C. after graduation. No job. Just a dream and a whole lot of faith."

"Landed at the Pentagon in a matter of weeks," Vivian said. "Ended up highest-ranking civilian under the Secretary of Defense."

"Isn't that where she met Captain Huntington?" Bertie asked. "That hunka-hunka burning love?"

"Bertie! You mean, *Admiral* Huntington," Lori Anne corrected.

"Five kids. Thirteen moves," Vivian said. "And still not that long ago, she was doing cannonballs into a hotel pool in her Easter dress."

"I couldn't do that," Lori Anne said.

"Or me," replied Mary Jo. "Or ride a camel in Jerusalem."

"She's the only person I know who'd hike Angel's Landing in a monogrammed windbreaker," added Viv.

"Hey, turn that up," Bertie said, joining them in the hall. "It's Miss Grace!"

"The Tams?" asked Lori Anne.

"The Tymes," Mary Jo answered. Thumbing her eyes, she said, "This is never going to work."

"What?" Viv asked.

"This! Us! Standing around talking about old times with Jackie." Swiping her eyes again, she added, "Now I'm going to have to do my makeup all over again."

Vivian reached around the doorframe of her room and produced a box. "Tissue?"

"Thanks." Sniffing, Lori Anne said, "I've spent a lot of money to look this way. I'll be danged if I'm going out with raccoon eyes."

"Sorry I brought it up," said Bertie.

"Hey, hey," Mary Jo replied. "This isn't on you. It's … well, we all knew it would …"

At the crunch of tires on the shell driveway, the four rushed into Vivian's room and peered out the window.

The red Fiat Spider pulled in and parked beside Lori Anne's Lexus. Admiral Bill, behind the wheel, unbuckled his seatbelt. Jackie in the passenger seat, a silk scarf tied neatly around her head, waved up.

They froze.

Vivian whispered, "So much for rule number one."

"Oh look!" Bertie blurted. "Jackie's wearing a scarf!"

Mary Jo's heart leapt. "Bertie, you can't act like you notice."

"How can I not? It's on her head."

"But it's rude."

"You don't think Jackie knows she's wearing a scarf?" Pushing up the window, Bertie yelled, "I love the color of that scarf! Makes your brown eyes pop." Taking a moment to look back at Mary Jo, she added, "And if I have my way, this weekend we'll all wear scarves to match our eyes."

"Come on," said Vivian. "Let's get this party started."

Three of them started toward the bedroom door.

"You coming?" Vivian asked.

"In a sec," Mary Jo answered. "I need a moment."

They drifted out, their chatter receding down the hallway.

Mary Jo sank onto the edge of the bed. In the mirror across from her, her reflection blinked back—smudged eyeliner, wilted curls, red at the corners of her eyes.

But it wasn't her own face she saw. It was her mother's. Tired. Worried. Trying to hold it all together with lipstick and a pressed blouse. A woman who never cried until everyone else was out of the room.

She could pretend.

Smile. Say the right things. Keep the party moving. Keep Jackie from seeing the wreckage behind her eyes.

Or ... she could break.

Let the tears come. Let Jackie know—really know—how much she mattered. Say the things that sat like hot stones in her chest, even if they spilled out cracked and trembling.

But this wheel of dread kept turning faster, meaner—pulling her thoughts into places she didn't want to go. The kind of dark corners where fear dressed up like logic and whispered lies. She hated herself for it. Hated that while Jackie was fighting for her life with grace and grit, she—Mary Jo—was spinning out in her own mind.

She knew better. She *was* getting better. She was on a path of healing, for heaven's sake. And this time, it wasn't grief. It was something heavier. A strange, looming shadow she couldn't name. A dark cloud of foreboding that settled over her spirit like weather she couldn't outrun.

She reached for the tissue box Vivian had left behind.

I'm choosing wounded. She stood and adjusted the neckline of her blouse. *But not broken.*

She left to join the others.

Chapter Eight

After Vivian got Jackie settled in her room, her watch pinged. "Oh my gosh. We were supposed to be at Paul's at Pawleys for dinner."

"When, Viv?" asked Lori Anne.

"Now!"

"Wait a minute," Mary Jo said, frowning. "We always go to Paul's on the second night."

Vivian looked at her, puzzled. "Mary Jo, it's always been the first night—since our very first trip. What's going on with you?"

Mary Jo stared at the group, her mind on Virginia as it had been all afternoon. Her daughter's silence tugged at her in the way that made small things—like what night they usually went to Paul's—slip past unnoticed. She shrugged. "A lot on my mind, is all. Must've mixed it up."

Lori Anne chuckled. "Well, we may be older, but some things will never change. We're late. Again."

They grabbed their purses, herded themselves into Vivian's Lincoln SUV, and took off in a choir of laughter, clicking seat belts, and a chaotic chorus of "Carolina girls, best in the world."

Mary Jo shifted in her seat, twisting the strap of her purse in her lap. The call from the accountant still echoed in her mind. Dry words, polite tone, but loaded with final probate instructions she wasn't ready to face. Charles had been gone for almost two years, yet his name on someone else's lips still made her breath catch. And now Virginia. That girl had always led with her heart, but this time something in her voice hadn't sounded right. Not giddy. Not even certain. Quiet. Heavy. Mary Jo pressed her fingers together, trying to squeeze the worry back into its corner.

She hadn't planned to say anything about Virginia's news. Not yet. But with the sky darkening and the girls laughing like they used to, the words pressed harder against her chest.

Vivian hit the gas. "If Arthur hadn't delivered Paul's daughter during an emergency C-section a few years back, we'd never have gotten this reservation, much less any grace to be late."

Jackie leaned in. "Speakin' of Arthur, how is he, Viv?"

"Fine, I guess. I'll give him a call later. But he's been swamped lately. Every one of my calls rolls straight to voicemail." Vivian gave a short laugh that didn't quite land. "You know Arthur, up to his elbows in some woman's private parts and calling it work."

"Gross!"

Vivian kept her eyes on the road, fingers tight on the wheel. "You asked, Jackie."

At Paul's, dinner lived up to its reputation—warm sourdough bread, perfect wine pairings—and not a scrap left behind, except on Mary Jo's plate.

Paul's hadn't changed. Still, the hush of linen-draped tables, the soft clink of glasses, the jazz trio crooning from the corner like they'd been hired in 1987 and never left. Candlelight floated in bowls of water on each table, flickering like tiny bonfires between friends. The scent of rosemary and broiled butter clung to the air, thick as memory. It was the kind of place where laughter held its breath, waiting to see if it still belonged.

"Mary Jo, you haven't touched your shrimp and grits," Jackie said. "And that's your favorite."

Mary Jo forced a smile. "Nibbled too much over drinks. I'll save the rest for later."

"Lawd, help, I'm stuffed." Lori Anne patted her stomach. "I haven't eaten this much since our Homecomin' Celebration. Did I tell y'all about the pineapple casserole incident?"

Four heads turned.

"I wanted to make a good first impression on the church ladies, so I made my famous pineapple casserole. I placed it right in the center of the main covered-dish table."

She let the silence stretch for dramatic effect.

"And no one touched it. Not one bite. Well, one brave soul tried a spoonful, bless her." She shook her head. "I was so rushed, I baked one of my girls' woven 4-H potholders right into the casserole. It looked ready for judging at the county fair. But at the church covered-dish? It won first place for stares and whispers."

Laughter spilled across the table.

"Sammie tried to play it off. Told folks I'd been sneakin' extra fiber into his diet. Got a few polite laughs, but some of those church ladies looked at me like I'd smuggled in deviled eggs straight from the devil himself." She shook her head, eyes wide. "I'm tellin' y'all, I don't think they've ever cracked a smile in their lives."

Vivian didn't miss a beat. "Suga, some of those church ladies are just old biddies. Been sittin' in the same pew so long they've laid eggs and started hatching drama. You keep being Lori Anne. Sooner or later, they'll crack all on their own."

Lori Anne sipped her sweet tea and leaned in. "Y'all, I stuck a sock over that smoke detector in my bedroom. I'm tellin' you, it's probably a spy cam. I read an article about how folks are watching strangers like it's cable TV. Well, they're not getting a free show from me!"

"Lori Anne, those are brand new smoke detectors. Arthur replaced them in January like he always does. It's a ritual with him."

"Still ... with so many workers in and out of the house, you never can be too sure."

"If it'll make you happy, I'll check the one in your room when we get back."

"And mine," said Jackie.

"Mine too," Bertie added.

"Mary Jo?"

"Um?"

"Yours too?"

"My what?"

"Forget it. Coffee and dessert anyone?"

Mary Jo waited for the cheesecake, tiramisu, key lime pie, and dark-chocolate cookies to arrive before saying, "Hey, y'all. I wanted to tell you something." The shift in her voice brought a hush to the table.

Vivian looked up. "Is something wrong, Mary Jo?"

She hesitated. "I don't think so. But it's about Virginia."

Jackie leaned in. "Is she sick?"

Mary Jo shook her head, giving a soft sigh. The concern on their faces made her heart ache a little. "No, nothing like that. She's, uh, found someone. Says she's in love, but she's said that before."

Bertie sat up straighter. "Well, that sounds like good news."

Mary Jo gave a small smile. "I hope so. I really do." She glanced around the table at her oldest friends. "It's just ... when I ask when I'm going to meet him, she's evasive. Honestly, I'm wondering if it's another woman."

"Virginia?" asked Lori Anne. "No way. She's straight as they come."

"These days, you never know," Mary Jo replied.

Vivian lifted her coffee cup. "To Virginia."

"And love," Jackie added.

The server returned to gather the remaining dishes. When Vivian asked for the check, he replied, "Already taken care of."

"What? By whom?"

"Not sure. Someone named Will? He called and gave his credit card number."

"You mean Bill?" Jackie asked.

"Yeah, maybe Bill. Said something about, 'My favorite SFG, especially Jackie, and to make sure y'all have fun.'"

The girls held up their cups again. "To *Will*."

"And love," Lori Anne said.

"And Virginia," Bertie said.

"We already toasted Virginia," Vivian said.

"We did?"

"To Bertie," Mary Jo said. "And the Second Floor Girls. Never give up. Never put out. Never say never."

"To the SFG," they said in unison.

Chapter Nine

Mary Jo had slipped off her sandals and cinched her terrycloth robe tight when the shriek of a smoke detector filled the living room. Sharp and jarring, the sound sliced through the beach house.

Vivian stood on a half ladder, hands barely reaching the ceiling and device. "No camera. Do you feel better, Lori Anne?"

"You can't be sure," Lori Anne called from upstairs. "Those things are small."

The detector continued its piercing *beep*, annoying and sudden.

"Looks like this one's the real deal," Vivian answered. She jammed it back into place. The beeping continued.

"Broken?" Mary Jo asked.

Vivian smacked it with her fist. The beeping stopped.

"Fixed."

Mary Jo eased down into the couch. The cushions exhaled beneath her, soft and sinking, like they understood the weight she carried. Her fingers found the rim of her wine glass, circling slow and deliberate, as if some answer might rise from the swirl. The old SFG game they started in college was winding its way back around. She could feel it tightening, pressing in from all sides.

A moment later another detector wailed.

Vivian gathered her ladder and called upstairs. "Lori Anne, is that you?"

"Have mercy, it's loud!"

"Plug it back in!" Vivian yelled.

"Trying."

"Y'all, enough with the detectors," Bertie said, voice flat. "If we wind up in a *Girls Gone Wild* video, so be it."

The screeching stopped.

"Let's do this later, can we?" asked Mary Jo. "It's killing my buzz."

Vivian propped the ladder against a wall. "It's only seven thirty. And y'all know what that means."

Mary Jo let out a groan that bounced off every bedroom door. "Oh, Lord."

Vivian raised her wine glass high. "Time for our first-night favorite game."

Mary Jo sank deeper into the couch, bracing herself. The air around Vivian crackled with the kind of energy that preceded a storm—or a setup.

Vivian clapped once. "Alright, the category is 'I Swear to Tell the Truth.'"

Lori Anne bounded down the steps wrapped in a lime green bathrobe that gave her the look of a lollipop. "Now, Viv, the Bible says it's not right to swear."

Vivian rolled her eyes so hard they nearly orbited the room. "Okay, Miss Holier Than Thou. We'll revise it. 'I Promise to Tell the Truth.' Happy now?"

"Much better," Lori Anne said, sipping spritzer water with saintly smugness.

Vivian grinned. "Wonderful. I've already tossed everyone's name in the bowl so we can keep this party goin'."

Mary Jo narrowed her eyes. *She's aiming straight at me,* she thought, as a third detector gave a short, dying chirp.

The five girls stared at the half-bath in the hallway.

"Mercy me," said Vivian. "I forgot. They're on a circuit. Mess with one, mess with all."

"Like us," said Jackie.

"Be right back. Arthur claims he's part electrician—his instructions are taped to the fuse box. I told him there's a difference between circuits and a cervix."

Laughter broke loose—sharp, sudden, and contagious.

"I'll start." Bertie dipped her hand into the bowl with the flourish of a game show host. "And the winner is … oh, would you look at this … Mary Jo!"

Mary Jo raised both hands. "This is a setup. And every last one of y'all knows it."

"Vivian's idea," Bertie said. "Now that you've been single for over two years, we figured it's time. Come on, Mary Jo, tell us what happened that night. You know the one—Folly Beach?"

Mary Jo's expression softened enough to give her away.

Lori Anne leaned forward, eyes wide. "Come on, honey. Confession is good for the soul."

The room stilled. Tension stretched thin, one word away from tearing.

"There. That should do it." Vivian walked back into the room.

Mary Jo caught Vivian's eye.

"You going first?" Vivian asked.

"You know I am."

"Okay, but before Mary Jo spills anything, it's time for The Pledge."

Mary Jo arched a brow. "Seriously, Vivian? The last time we did The Pledge was our senior year of college."

Vivian straightened her shoulders. "I think it's high time we resurrected it for such a time as this."

All eyes swung to Mary Jo. She sighed, the weight of tradition—or mischief—settling in. "Fine. Just to make it official, I brought our CWC senior yearbook. If we're doing The Pledge, I'll get the book." She disappeared for a few minutes, then returned with the prized relic, cradling it like it was the holy grail of the Second Floor Girls. Lifting her pinky with a look equal parts solemn and sassy, she began, "I pinky promise, under the entirely fictitious bylaws of the Second Floor Girls, to tell the whole truth, nothing but the truth—"

Bertie chuckled. "I believe I've heard those words before."

Laughter bubbled around the room, soft and warm.

Then the hallway alarm gave a quick shriek, but no more.

"They're possessed," said Lori Anne.

"Suga, that was your idea," Vivian replied. "Cast 'em out."

Mary Jo sipped her wine, steadying herself. "Alright," she said. "I'll tell y'all what happened."

Chairs creaked. The others froze, breathless.

"It was the summer between our sophomore and junior years," Mary Jo began, her thumb tracing the curve of her glass. "Y'all know I dropped Spanish twice. Couldn't pass it to save my life. So Momma and Daddy let me move to Charleston for summer school. Took it at College of Charleston. Some cousins rented a place on Folly, so we split the cost."

She paused, grin tugging. All eyes focused on her.

"One morning, I went out for a jog. Only clean swimsuit I had was this hideous yellow-beige thing that matched my skin. No cover-up."

"Camouflage couture," Lori Anne offered.

"Exactly," Mary Jo laughed. "This guy runs past me, stops dead, turns, and says, 'Wow! I thought I'd stumbled onto a nude beach.'"

The girls howled.

"He had the thickest Northern accent and, oh boy, he was a looker. Blue-green eyes, perfect tan, abs you could do laundry on."

"You mean like a washboard?" Jackie asked.

"No, sculpted. Divine. We walked for miles, talked forever. His name was Ted, and he was in town for some tech conference."

"Oh, Lord." Vivian groaned. "Here we go. Hold on to your hormones—or what's left of them."

"We split a Coke and sat at the Pavilion. But I was still in that swimsuit, and folks were staring. Ted finally bought me one of those wraparound sarongs. Thank the Lord. Before that, people probably thought I'd walked out there buck naked."

More laughter.

"We watched the sunset, and I forgot all about class. I mean, I was smitten."

Vivian edged closer. "And then?"

Mary Jo clasped her hands, eyes wide. "When the sun went down, we ducked behind the biggest sand dune and started making out."

Lori Anne gasped. "You can't stop there!"

"Well," said Jackie, "Did you stop?"

Mary Jo held up a hand. "Y'all are so bad."

"You swore," Vivian said.

"No," Lori Anne corrected. "You promised."

Mary Jo sighed. "Fine. Things got real cozy. Ted looked at me and said, 'You better stop me now.' I didn't."

A long pause ensued.

"Then bam—headlights. A flashlight cut through the dark. Blinded me. My cousins had called the Folly Beach police. They'd been looking for me for hours."

Gasps echoed.

"So did you do it?" Jackie asked.

Mary Jo looked toward the window. "No. Folly Beach police saved more than my reputation. I remained ... uh ... pure but not innocent."

Vivian stood. "Lawd have mercy, I need a cigarette."

Bertie leaned forward. "Did you ever see him again?"

Mary Jo nodded. "I invited him to meet my parents. I thought maybe he was *The One*. But Momma—y'all knew her—she took one look and said, 'So, Ted, do you eat fish on Fridays?'"

"She was fishin'," muttered Vivian.

"Exactly. After he left, she pulled me aside and said, 'Really, Mary Jo? No one in this family from the Church of England, Episcopalian, has ever considered marrying a Yankee, much less a Roman Catholic.'"

Jackie exhaled. "I've spent a lifetime in rooms where I wasn't welcome."

Bertie sat taller. "Gracious, Jackie, we've loved you since the first time I introduced you to the SFG."

The room went still.

Vivian narrowed her eyes. "Hold on. This Roman Catholic Ted ... does he have a last name?"

"Silvain."

Jackie blinked. "Ted *Silvain*? The tech guy?"

Mary Jo took a slow sip of her drink. "Mmm-hmm."

Jackie nearly choked. "He's the CEO of Nexi—one of the biggest tech companies in the world. I heard he bought The Indigo Room on King Street, next to the King Charles' Place."

Vivian said, "Get out! I love The Indigo Room."

Mary Jo smiled gently. "Now y'all know I loved Charles. That man took care of me. We didn't have fireworks, but we had groceries paid, oil changed, and a porch light that always worked."

Lori Anne sighed. "I guess you can find romance in reliable lighting and fresh motor oil."

Mary Jo tucked a strand of hair behind her ear. She took a deep breath, then the words drifted out like a slow breeze across the water. "But before all that, Ted and I shared a Coke, a scorcher of a day, and one night under the stars I'll never forget. And those blue-green eyes? The ocean's never looked the same."

A hard knock rattled the front door.

All five women jumped up. Bare feet padded over wood floors. Robes cinched. Hands snatched pillows to cover breasts.

Vivian hurried to the door with the dignity of a woman who had silenced a beeping smoke detector with her bare fist—and perhaps, Mary Jo thought, broken some security circuit in the process. The other women gathered in the foyer. From her angle, Mary Jo caught sight of red lights, flashing low and slow across the windows of the homes across the street.

Fire truck. Great.

Vivian swung open the back-porch door, revealing six feet of prime Carolina muscle in a fireman's jacket and cargo pants, standing under their porch light.

A deep male voice said, "Evening, ma'am. Everything okay? We got a call about a fire at this address."

Vivian stammered. "Oh, no, it was a smoke alarm, I mean, several. False alarms, we think."

"No false alarms, ma'am. I'm detecting a goodly amount of heat."

"You sure?" Vivian asked. "I don't—"

"But that's okay. Some like it hot." Without another word, the man bent, pressed a button on a black boom box at his feet, and the porch filled with the pulsing beat of "Some Like It Hot" by Power Station. He began to gyrate his hips to the beat of the music.

Mary Jo blinked. The porch lights flickered. Lori Anne gasped. Bertie walked toward the open door.

Jackie whispered what they were all thinking. "Y'all ... did Vivian hire a stripper?"

The boom box thumped louder.

Abandoning their cover, the girls moved closer to enjoy the show.

Lori Anne crossed herself—wrong, but with conviction. "Girl, my hormones are doing the hokey pokey. Lord, forgive me ... but don't stop!"

Vivian snorted. "Hallelujah! Looks like Lori Anne's havin' her own personal revival!"

Chapter Ten

One by one, the women stepped outside, barefoot and quiet, drawn by a morning that asked nothing and offered everything. The Atlantic pushed light ashore in ribbons, each wave tugging the sun a little higher. The porch creaked beneath their rockers, the fresh boards still settling in. Through the open windows, the house exhaled the warmth of coffee into the salt-stirred air.

Mary Jo cradled her mug, eyes on the edge of the surf where the sun split the water into gold and shadow. The coffee warmed her palms, but something else had stirred up the morning—an unease she felt as she awoke.

"I know y'all think it was Bill." Jackie's voice was light but riding the edge of something sharper. "But that man can't even book a dentist appointment without me walking him through the website. Yet somehow he hires an exotic dancer in leather chaps and a firehose so long …"

"Part of me feels guilty. The other part's still smiling like I got away with something naughty," Lori Anne said, biting her lip. "Jackie, that man of yours loves you."

Jackie shook her head, her half-smile curling upward. "I'm touched, I guess. But I swear, sometimes he tries too hard, if you know what I mean."

Bertie leaned forward, squinting. "Better he pays attention and cares than not. I hope if I ever get—"

"Don't say it," Lori Anne said. "We'll be there for you, Bertie. We'll be there for all of us."

Mary Jo kept her mouth shut. Watching. Listening.

Tugging her robe tight, Vivian said, "I don't think I've slept that good in months."

"Probably the wine," Mary Jo said.

"Or the stripper," Bertie added.

"Mercy, Mary Jo. That story you told last night curled my toes," said Lori Anne. "Better than any Harlequin romance I've ever hidden in a church bulletin."

Mary Jo smiled. She wanted the group to hold together—fragile as they were, with Bertie growing more forgetful and Jackie frailer than ever. What they needed was simple: peace. The kind of peace and restoration that only their beach time could provide.

"It was a long time ago, but I still think about Ted."

Bertie narrowed her eyes at the horizon. "Ted who?"

Mary Jo hesitated for a beat, then shifted her tone. "Oh, you remember Ted, don't you? If not, remind me later and I'll fill you in."

"Oh, Ted, sure. We went by his house yesterday."

"We did?" asked Vivian.

"Yeah. You pointed it out. 'There's where Ted talks.' Big ugly house that looked like a pat of butter."

Lori Anne reached over, patting Bertie's hand. "That was Lana Crenshaw's place."

"Oh, that's right," Bertie replied. "Home smells like yeast and regrets."

"Okay, y'all, after all the excitement from last night, I think we need a devotion. I have my Bible," said Lori Anne.

"Do we have a choice?" asked Vivian.

"Yes." Mary Jo shot Vivian a hard look. "I agree with Lori Anne. "We probably need to add a few Sunday school lessons too, since we all acted like adolescent school girls."

"I promise this'll bless your heart. I've got notes highlighted in four colors and the whole outline printed from that Faith,

Fashion, and Fellowship breakout session. I prayed on it, planned it, and tucked it neatly inside my prized Louis Vuitton Bible case. Now where did I put it?"

"Louis?" Jackie asked.

"Louis holding King James," said Vivian with a smirk. Next thing you know, Chanel'll be leadin' Bible studies and Coach'll be takin' prayer requests."

"Oh, excuse me for a minute." Without warning, Bertie shot up from her rocker. "There's something I need to do."

Mary Jo continued sipping her coffee until … "Good gracious alive," she said, cringing. "What's that smell?"

"Banana bread," Bertie yelled. "I'm on breakfast duty, remember?"

"Oh, dear Lord," said Vivian. "She's burned it."

"That"—said Lori Anne, standing and sniffing—"is not banana bread. That's charred leather."

The four rushed into the kitchen to find Bertie standing proudly at the oven, potholder in hand. She yanked open the oven door.

The blast of heat hit them first, then the sight of something blackened and bubbling resting on the center rack.

"Lori Anne's Louis Vuitton Bible case," Jackie said in a hushed whisper.

Charred. Melted. Still faintly smoking. Mary Jo took the potholder from Bertie and carefully slid the rack out. Lifting the blackened lump, she placed Lori Anne's Bible, encased in a melted black blob, in the sink.

"King James has gone straight to glory, but it looks like Louis Vuitton has gone to hell," Vivian said.

"Not funny," Lori Anne replied.

"Come on, Lori Anne," Vivian said. "Chapter and verse. Where does it say that the Word of God is a consuming fire?"

Lori Anne forced a smile. "I guess you could say it's the hottest thing Louis has ever made."

"Bertie, you've outdone yourself," said Vivian. "Holy Smoked Banana Surprise. Who would have thought you could remember the recipe?"

With a butter knife, Mary Jo prodded and poked at the Bible. "It's not as bad as it looks, Lori Anne. The cover is messed up, but not all that much."

"I'm so sorry." Bertie's lower lip trembled.

"Hey, hey! No tears," Vivian said. "This is nothing. Isn't that right, Lori Anne? Lori Anne?"

"Yes, right. Not a biggie. Collector's item, but I can get another one, sure."

Mary Jo's phone chirped. After glancing at the screen she looked up at Vivian. "Viv, any idea why Arthur is texting me?"

"He is?"

"He's asking if we got his big surprise." Mary Jo swiped the screen. "Oh ... I see." She held up the phone for all to see.

"*He* ... sent the stripper?" Vivian huffed. "He won't talk to me, but he sends a stripper?"

"At least he's thinking of you," Jackie said.

"Look at us in that picture," Vivian said. "We look trashed—our entertainer had a body cam. I can hear Arthur now: *Girls Gone Wild: The Menopausal Years.*"

"Only you look trashed, Viv," Mary Jo said. "I'm still wearing my makeup. He wants an answer. How should I respond?"

"Answer to what?" Vivian asked. "Just tell him I'll be callin' Paulie, our local mobster. That'll send a message louder than a porch stripper in broad daylight."

"I'll say ..." Mary Jo began typing.

"What? What are you going to say?"

"You'll see." Mary Jo dropped her phone into the pocket of her robe. "We better get dressed."

"We goin' somewhere?" asked Bertie.

"Out."

"But where?" Bertie asked.

"Gracious, let's just go anywhere," Mary Jo said, waving her hand.

"I think the SFG just produced their first Hallmark film—steamy romance, a porch stripper, and a King James Bible that went up in flames." Lori Anne grinned. "I'll tell you what. If the church biddies ever see this, they'll be cluckin' and layin' eggs for sure!"

Chapter Eleven

Brunch at their favorite dive—part restaurant, part shrine to bad decisions. Making menu decisions included mimosas served in glass flutes and the sound of silverware clanging against china, an oddly elegant sound for an open-air cafe looking down on the waterway.

After a second round of drinks, bread baskets disappeared. Salads arrived.

"So ... Arthur?" Jackie started. "What's up with that?"

"What do you mean?" Vivian asked.

"You said you called, left a message, left texts, but he's not responding."

"That's Arthur. You could say sending the stripper was quite revealing. I'm not worried. Georgia is. He's supposed to send her money for her car payment and hasn't."

A chocolate dessert, sinful and towering, landed in the center of the table. Five spoons attacked without concern for equal distribution.

"No comment from him about the stripper?" Lori Anne asked.

"I think he's ticked that I wasn't getting a lap dance. So like him. Sleaze and tease."

"Wish I had a little sleaze in my life," Jackie said. "Hard to feel sexy after a round of chemo."

With a forced smile, their server dropped off the check.

Vivian slid her glasses onto her nose. "We need the check split. Dessert is on me."

The waiter gave an apologetic smile. "Sorry. For parties of five or more, it's one check."

"That's crazy."

"Policy, ma'am."

Mary Jo grabbed a pen from her purse. "I can figure it out. Let's see, Bertie you had the Cobb salad and Lori Anne, yours was—"

"Oh, for heaven's sake," Vivian interrupted. "Just divide it by five and the four of you can Venmo me the money."

"Won't work," Mary Jo said, scribbling numbers on a napkin. "Not all of us use apps that track our spending. We're splitting it all—tip included, right?"

"We do this dance every time we eat out," Jackie said.

"We do?" asked Bertie.

"Fifteen or twenty percent?" Mary Jo asked.

"Service was decent." Jackie reached for the last muffin crumb. "Fifteen seems fair."

"Fifteen? That's all?" Vivian raised a brow. "That boy's probably putting himself through college."

"No way," Lori Anne said. "Boy like him with looks like that, he's from money. His haircut alone is close to a hundred dollars. But tip whatever you want. Doesn't matter. At this rate, I'll be broke before we even hit the clearance rack tomorrow."

"I'll cover Lori Anne," Bertie offered, reaching for her purse—and finding it missing.

"Where's your bag, Bertie?"

"I had it … when we came in. I remember putting on lipstick while you four were looking at the funny greeting cards."

"That was at The Shop at Pawleys."

Jackie asked, "Mary Jo? You need a calculator?"

"Almost got it."

"Oh, Lord." Lori Anne chuckled. "We're gonna be here till supper."

"I could have sworn those greeting cards were up by the cash register," Bertie said.

Vivian paid the bill and with scraps of napkin, Mary Jo doled out collection payments to the other three. "Venmo me," she said under her breath to Vivian. "Sounds like something that shouldn't be spoken of in public."

"Your mind goes to the gutter faster than any woman I know," Vivian replied.

"It's hell living alone, Viv. Try it sometime, you'll see."

Unlocking the car, Vivian asked, "What say we swing by Sandy's?"

A groan rose from the group.

"Not Push-Up Sandy," Lori Anne protested, fanning herself with a coupon. "Her cleavage is under her chin."

"Do we have to?" Jackie asked. "That shop smells of melted potpourri and looks like generational trauma in Capri pants."

"Doesn't matter to me one way or the other," said Bertie. "But I would like to find my purse."

"Oh, right, that," Vivian said. "We'll hit The Shop at Pawleys on the way. I'm surprised you didn't mention it sooner. If I'd lost my purse, I'd be in a panic."

"My panics come and go," Bertie answered.

"That woman dresses like she's still auditioning for the Miss Shrimp & Grits Pageant," Lori Anne said.

"Bertie?"

"No, Sandy."

Jackie didn't miss a beat. "Says the woman who once wore rhinestone wedges to a funeral."

"God's always watching. And when the Rapture comes, I want to meet up with my people in the sky looking fan-tab-u-lous."

"If she finds out we were down for our normal weekend and didn't stop in …"

"She'll add us back to her Christmas letter under *naughty*," Vivian said, "and Arthur thinks she looks hot as Mrs. Santa."

"Sad to say, but most guys—"

"Found it!" Passenger door open, Bertie bent over the back seat. Holding up her purse, she said, "Told you it was in the car."

No one spoke for a moment.

Bertie continued cheerfully, "Let's go see Sandy."

The others, still staring, opened doors and scrunched into the car.

"Bertie," Jackie said gently, "you do remember Sandy's place, right?"

"Of course. I'm not stupid. She's the one with all those porcelain cats."

"No, suga," Vivian said softly. "That's your Aunt Margie."

"Well, I like cats."

They turned into the tiny gravel lot, the familiar sign swinging crookedly in the breeze: *Sandy's Treasured Fashions & More*. The *more* had always been up for interpretation.

While the other four headed up the steps to Sandy's, Vivian said, "I'll be right back. I'm going to check on Arthur's chair."

"Chair?" Lori Anne asked.

The others looked at Palmetto Designs and pivoted at once. "So *that's* why you wanted to go to Sandy's."

"No, I swear. I didn't even think about that stupid chair until just now. Won't take but a sec."

The owner of Palmetto Designs came running out, smiling widely. "Ah, Mrs. Knox. I was about to call you. Your recliner came in just like you ordered. We'll be more than happy to deliver it any time. I think Dr. Knox is going to love it. It's in the back room. I'll be happy to show you."

Arthur's recliner. Custom-designed. Completes his precious study. She had sent Arthur so many links, fabric swatches, texts about look and style that he'd finally said, "How hard can it be to buy a chair, Viv? Just do it!"

"Let me check with my husband on delivery times, okay?"

"Sure. I'll wait to hear from you."

Vivian joined the other four on the front porch of Sandy's store. The door jingled, announcing their arrival.

Sandy called, "Hey ladies!" her voice thick and falsetto sweet. "Beach weekend, right?" She pivoted to point to a wall calendar with a circle around four squares. "I always mark your beach weekends right next to hurricane season—since, truth be told, y'all usually blow in just weeks apart."

"How nice," said Lori Anne.

Vivian's phone chirped. "It's Georgia. I'd better take this."

Sandy clapped her hands. "Y'all have got to see our wide-leg jeans. Only eighty-eight dollars! So retro seventies!"

"Vivian?" Lori Anne teased, "you're into retro, aren't you?"

"I know, I know. Don't panic, sweetie. Your daddy'll send the money. He always does." Holding her phone by her side, Vivian asked, "What size should I try?"

Sandy's eyes scanned Vivian from head to toe with the enthusiasm of someone appraising a side of beef. "Let's start with the largest and work our way down ... if we need to."

The group chuckled.

"You laugh," Vivian said softly. "You're next. What? No, sweetie, I wasn't saying it was something to laugh about. I was ..."

Sandy held a pair in front of Vivian. *Push-Up Sandy,* Vivian thought. *Queen of compliments with a PhD in Southern snark.*

"Sweetie, let me call you right back." Vivian stepped into the changing room and dialed Arthur. Voicemail. She left a message: "Call me back." She slipped off her shorts and into the jeans. Emerging, she tugged at the waistband. "Well?"

Sandy tilted her head. "Oh, D'lin, those jeans are just precious ... on someone much younger."

Witch.

Jackie grabbed a colorful top from the rack. "Alright, my turn. Let's see what kind of fashion statement I'll make in this top." She twirled in front of the mirror. "Tah-dah!"

Sandy beamed. "Now that is adorable on you, Jackie. And it would be even more adorable if it covered your hips."

Mary Jo mouthed, C-R-A-Z-Y

Jackie froze mid-spin, hands still in the air. "Well, if it's on sale …" She folded the top and placed it back on the table. "I just might—"

"Sandy, do y'all still carry those scented drawer liners?" Mary Jo asked. "My Aunt Frances loves those."

Sandy lit up. "Oh yes. We've got magnolia, gardenia, and camellia. Follow me!"

The girls fanned out behind her. Like ducklings, Vivian thought, waddling past mannequins draped in bold prints and questionable fringe behind the Wicked Witch of the Worst Manners Ever.

Once Sandy disappeared down an aisle, Vivian grabbed Jackie's elbow. "That hip comment. So out of line."

"It's okay. She doesn't know."

"Hell, she doesn't. That's just Sandy. One more snide comment from her, and I'm gonna need therapy, Spanx, and two strong men to hold me back."

Behind them, Lori Anne held up a pair of beaded flip-flops. "Y'all, these are twenty-five dollars and already missin' rhinestones."

Vivian glanced toward the front. Sandy was still talking to herself in the drawer liner section.

"Alright. We've shown our faces. Time to leave." Vivian adjusted her purse strap like a general about to issue orders. "We buy one item. Something under ten dollars. We smile. We lie about what a great shop this is. We run."

Jackie grabbed a dusty candle marked $6.99. "Found my ticket out of here."

Lori Anne clutched a jar of bath salts that smelled vaguely of regret and menthol. "Got mine."

They regrouped at the counter just as Sandy returned, drawer liners in hand and praise locked and loaded. "You girls are such a joy! I swear, it means the world when old friends stop by. Now listen, y'all aren't leavin' until each of you scans this QR code. I've got prize drawings, fashion tips, contests, and just enough laugh-out-loud photos of my customers doing stupid stuff to keep you snort-laughing through the week. Trust me, you don't wanna miss what's comin' your way!"

Vivian nodded, credit card and phone out. "Wouldn't miss it for the world."

Once they escaped to the parking lot, Vivian texted Arthur. "Good news. Your chair's ready. I'm at the store, and she wants to know when to deliver. Text me back."

When the four reached the car, Lori Anne gasped. "Oh, Lord, we left Bertie inside. Mary Jo?"

"I'll save her. Have mercy …would someone explain to me why we go to Sandy's every year?"

Vivian's phone chirped with a text from Arthur. *I'm working. Can I have a moment here?*

"A moment? You can have all the idiotic moments you want!"

Chapter Twelve

The Second Floor Girls rolled back into the house, shoes off and feet dragging.

Mary Jo stepped over the threshold and felt the cool hush of the house wrap around her. She exhaled, grateful to be out of the heat, her joints aching in a way she refused to name. The air conditioner hummed like a lullaby, and the scent of repurposed wood, salt, and something faintly lemony greeted her. She watched Bertie shuffle toward the kitchen and Jackie ease onto the couch. Vivian lingered by the door, face tight, fingers hovering near her phone.

Mary Jo sank into the nearest chair and lifted her legs with a groan. "I don't know about y'all, but the last thing I want to do is eat out. I'm flat worn out, again."

"Same," said Jackie. "Let's put on PJs, grab the leftovers, junk food, and sit around the den. That work for everybody?"

"We could go bar hopping," Lori Anne chimed in, wiggling her brows. "Just like y'all did to me the month before graduation?"

The room exploded with a collective laugh.

Jackie's phone dinged. She glanced down, then groaned. "Oh, Lord. Sandy emailed us."

"Already?" Mary Jo asked. "It's been what? An hour since we left?"

"Oh, I see. She's using the security footage from out front of the store," Jackie said, swiping the screen.

"Oh, for goodness sake," Lori Anne said, leaning over to see Jackie's phone. "She titled our visit: *Fashion Emergency: Five Lives in Ruin*."

The others crowded around as Jackie held up the screen.

There they were. Caught mid-slog, disheveled and half-melted, looking every bit like refugees from a senior citizens' shopping spree gone sideways. Bertie's visor sat crooked, and Mary Jo's shirt was inside out.

Vivian said, "I look like I just escaped a hostage situation involving scarves."

The caption read: *These five didn't roll out of the recliner lookin' fabulous, but Sandy's is about to fix that with sequins and Southern charm.*

Lori Anne squinted. "She used the fish-eye lens on purpose."

Bertie replied, "And we're her catch of the day."

Vivian refilled her wine glass. "She used that recliner line on purpose, don't you think?"

Mary Jo backed away, returning to her seat. "Let's change and take this party to the porch. Cooler out there than in here. Just like old times."

A sudden *boom* cracked through the air. The porch lights went out. So did the streetlamps.

Bertie gasped. "What in heaven …"

Darkness engulfed them, thick and complete.

"Transformer," Vivian said, matter of fact.

"I'll grab the other bottle of pinot grigio and a corkscrew," said Jackie.

The wind off the ocean slipped around them like a whisper from the past. Mary Jo pulled her cardigan tighter as she settled into the corner rocker. The porch creaked under their weight, groaning like it remembered them, like it had aged and bent too. The scent of salt clung to the air, mixing with leftover Brie, candle smoke, and something faintly medicinal—probably whatever Bertie had rubbed into her knees. Through the palms, the moon peeked out, silvering the deck rail and lighting the sea oats in flickers of light. Somewhere down the beach, wind chimes answered the call of distant waves.

They passed around wine, snacks, and one of Lori Anne's icy Diet Cokes.

Mary Jo stared toward the dark, moonlit horizon, the breeze lifting her hair. "That was *the* trip," she said softly. "The one we'll never forget."

No one needed to ask. The SFG knew exactly what she meant.

Vivian raised her glass with a sly smile. "To our amazing Southern mommas who brought us into this world … and threatened to take us out if we embarrassed them."

"To wearing lipstick to the mailbox and sweet tea that could soothe a broken heart," Mary Jo added.

"To pearls, prayers, and the dreaded discipline switch behind the living room door," said Jackie.

"And to the ones who laughed and gave us that I-told-you-so look," Vivian said.

They clinked glasses. Even Bertie's hand was steady.

"That was the year Arthur bought up half the condos at the Water's Edge," Vivian said.

Jackie nodded. "Felt less like a girls' trip and more like checking into a Marriott."

Vivian rolled her eyes. "I had to beg my mother to come. She almost didn't make it because she didn't want to leave her soft ice."

Mary Jo turned. "Soft ice?"

"She said no beach was worth giving up her fancy chewable ice from the corner gas station."

"My mother said she wasn't climbing to the third floor," Jackie added. "Said, 'If there's a fire, I'm not burning up in a beach condo.'"

"Oh please"—Lori Anne waved her Diet Coke—"mine said, 'I'm not spending the weekend with a bunch of old women in elastic pants.'"

The porch shook with laughter.

Vivian wiped her eyes. "And yet every one of them came anyway."

"So who gave the mommas Jell-O shots?"

Mary Jo raised her hand. "They were sittin' in 340 like they'd been sentenced. Arms crossed, lips zipped."

"Until ten minutes later, when my mother pulled out four decks of cards—cutthroat Canasta," Vivian said.

"And kicked us out for disrupting their concentration," Jackie added.

"The next morning, my car was gone," Jackie continued. "Turns out they hijacked it to hit those glittery beach stores."

"They came back with 'swimsuits,'" Vivian said, using air quotes.

Mary Jo nearly choked. "And there she was—my mother—riding the waves in a yellow shower cap."

"They needed Depends and two more oxygen tanks," Lori Anne said. "Momma said she laughed so hard she tinkled and blew through both tanks. No wonder Momma was the first one down and the last one to leave every night during revival. She stayed at the altar through every verse of 'Just As I Am.' Apparently, she needed absolution and air."

"Y'all know that prissy diva next door wouldn't speak to me after our mommas visited the condo," Vivian said.

"Oh, hush." Mary Jo grinned. "Who in their right mind would snub our fabulous Viv?"

"Well, I would've." Vivian sipped, then added, "After what my mother said when that diva walked by."

Jackie held up a hand. "And let's be honest, girls … as we age and keep shopping, our clothes oughta match both our figure and our face."

Lori Anne crossed her arms. "Not me. I can assure you this face and this body will remain fabulous 'til the Lord takes me home."

"Y'all hush," protested Mary Jo. "Viv's in the middle of her story. Go on, sweetie."

Vivian grinned. "So our mommas were all parked on the porch, sipping and spectating. I can still see Momma in her cat-eye sunglasses with the rhinestones sparkling. I knew right then she was fixin' to tell a story. Y'all know sound carries across water." She paused for effect. "That condo diva next door strutted by on the other side of the pool, and Momma squinted and said, 'Lord, that woman's wearin' a duck dress.' One of the others asked, 'Duck dress? I didn't see any ducks on that thing.' Momma said loud enough for all to hear, 'Aw, hell no. That dress is so short, it's up to her quack.'"

The girls howled.

"Dang, I hope that woman's not still living next door at the condos," Mary Jo said.

Viv waved her off. "Suga, she moved to The Villages. Bought a house with a yard full of plastic flamingos and no shame. Have mercy, that woman loved men."

"Truth is," said Jackie, "my momma scared the hell out of me. She met some old man on that same trip. Every sunset, he'd drive her down to The Point in his fancy golf cart."

"I'm not even going to ask if your momma told you what they did," said Lori Anne.

Vivian nodded. "As if we need details."

Chuckling at the mental image of Jackie's mom and a strange man next door to their condo parking at The Point and …

"Thanks," Bertie said. ""Now I've got that image of the golf cart a rockin' and those two—"

"Don't finish that thought," said Lori Anne.

"Too late," Mary Jo chimed in. "It's already burned in my brain."

Vivian looked up. "Oh, that was Henry Brooks. He lived in 342. I swear, he loved that pimped-out cart more than most people love their pets."

Jackie asked, "What did you say his name was?"

"Henry. Henry Brooks. Why?"

Jackie stared straight ahead. "Well, that explains it."

"What does?" Lori Anne asked.

Jackie lowered her voice. "When Momma got sick, she stayed in bed most of the time. We knew it was the end. The hospice nurse told me she was transitioning."

"You mean dying," Lori Anne said.

Jackie nodded slowly. "She started mumbling. Then, outta nowhere, she sat up in bed—eyes wide—and shouted, 'I'm coming! I'm coming!' I thought she was seeing Daddy until the third time, when she said it louder, 'I'm coming … Henry!'"

"Wasn't your daddy's name George?" Bertie asked.

"Uh, yeah. Now you're getting it," said Jackie. "And I guess Momma had been too."

The porch erupted with laughter.

Jackie grew quiet. Her eyes, bright just moments before, drifted to the edge of the porch where the shadows were thickest. "You know, that was about the only time Momma let slip how reckless she used to be. It changed how I saw her. It was also about the last thing she ever told me. Because right after—" She covered her face and sobbed.

Vivian reached over, her comfort automatic. "Oh, Jackie. We didn't mean to—"

"No, that's not it," Jackie said, between hiccupping sniffles. "It's …" Thumbing her eyes, she looked up and steadied herself. "The chemo's not working."

Her words cut straight through the hush and the slap of surf, ripping through Mary Jo's heart.

"They said it might shrink the tumor. It hasn't."

The other four folded in upon her, forming a shelter. Vivian and Mary Jo dropped to a knee. Bertie and Lori Anne leaned in.

"I sat for hours while poison dripped into my body. Trying to imagine it was killing the cancer, but all it did was leave me exhausted, sick, and so sore my fingernails ache. My skin's so thin I bruise from hugs."

They started to pull away.

"No, don't! Please, stay around me!"

The huddle reformed, tighter and wet with tears. Sniffles mixed with Jackie's choking sobs.

When at last Mary Jo thought her friend was spent, Jackie said, "I lie in bed at night praying I'll make it to our next beach trip."

Another spasm of emotion erupted, pushing aside the petty worries Mary Jo wanted to share but could not.

"I haven't told Bill. He still kisses my bald head as if I'm pretty. But when I get home, I have to tell him. We'll cry together. Then I'll make cornbread, and he'll put on Motown like he always does. And when I can find the strength to carry him through this, we'll make plans for what comes next."

"Oh, Jackie," sobbed Bertie. "My sweet, beautiful Jackie. This is so not fair."

Jackie cleared her throat. "But tonight, I need y'all to surround me. Laugh with me. Help me forget what's coming. Can you do that?"

Silence settled over the SFG.

"Mary Jo, I need to ask you something. You're single, and ... well ... when the time comes, I ... um ... Bill ..."

Mary Jo squinted. "Wait. Are you seriously asking me to get together with your husband after—"

Jackie winced. "I guess ..."

Mary Jo met her eyes. "Absolutely not. I don't know how to ride a camel … in Jerusalem!"

Lori Anne added without missing a beat, "And let's not forget Jesus rode a donkey."

That did it. The Second Floor Girls lost it—snorts, howls, and laughter all around.

Jackie wiped a tear and grinned. "Okay, ladies. I needed that."

Vivian forced a smile, then moved to the railing. She stared out at the dark, wine in hand.

Mary Jo reached for the wine bottle, then froze. At the end of the boardwalk a man mounted the steps and began walking toward the house.

"Ladies," Mary Jo said. "We've got company."

"Maybe it's another stripper," said Lori Anne, running to see the new intruder.

From the walkway, the man called, "Either of you Vivian Knox? I'm with the Horry County Sheriff's Department. I have a summons for a Mrs. Arthur Knox."

Chapter Thirteen

As Vivian stepped onto the porch the next morning, wind tugged at the edges of her windbreaker, the air colder than it had any right to be in May. A faint crust of salt clung to the deck rail, its grit a small reminder that even time and tide could take the edge off worry.

Maybe Arthur had been distant because of another summons—a deposition in yet another wrongful death suit. Frivolous, yes. Arthur had faced baseless accusations before. But the last time, *she* got dragged into it—into his world of lawyers, settlements, and skyrocketing insurance premiums. *This* had to be the reason he wasn't answering her texts or sounded frustrated when she called. Arthur always tried to protect her.

She scanned the shoreline where clouds stacked like unspoken regrets, masking the horizon. The sun lay out there somewhere, hidden under the hush of gray.

Reaching the end of the walkway, she took Jackie's hand, steadying her as her friend stepped onto the sand.

"Well, so much for our postcard morning." Vivian zipped her jacket, sealing herself in. "I should go back to the kitchen and fix myself a Bloody Mary. That's my mood right now."

"So early? Never mind. Not my business." Jackie took a quick look east, then trudged on. "I don't mind the gray. Means we get the beach to ourselves." She tapped her watch. "I've got 5,342 steps already this weekend. My goal's fifteen thousand before I go home."

Vivian raised an eyebrow. "You planning to jog to Charleston and back?"

Jackie smiled. "Girl, I'm planning to get so far ahead of this disease it'll never catch me—or at least make it work up a sweat."

Viv decided the Bloody Mary could wait. The morning felt too fragile to drown it in vodka and tomato juice. They crossed through the dunes, gulls shrieking and wheeling overhead. A couple in matching visors passed by with wide, performative grins. Vivian nodded, but her smile failed to lift her heart. In their wake, crumbs from a bagel attracted terns and pipers. "Same boardwalk, different year. The sand between my toes feels good. Feels good to put one foot in front of the other."

"Viv," Jackie said, voice softer now, "you don't know how true that statement is."

They walked in silence, the wind lifting the edge of Jackie's ball cap like it might carry it off. The beach, always their friend, now seemed a little too eager to whip them with sand, slinging salt spray against cool cheeks.

"I used to walk this stretch wondering if I could get my thighs to stop jiggling," Jackie said, chuckling. "Now? I thank God I've got legs that'll carry me through another day."

Vivian gave her a look. "You sure you're okay to be out here this early?"

Jackie shrugged. "I've got a port in my chest, a head full of peach fuzz, and a calendar with no more appointments circled. I'm not missing a single sunrise."

Vivian took her friend's hand and gave it a squeeze. "From my heart to yours."

Silence. Steps. The squawk of a solitary gull winging over the surf.

"I know y'all are worried," Jackie said, voice level. "Me too."

Vivian swallowed hard. "I hate this part where we all have to act brave."

Jackie nodded. "It's not about being brave anymore. It's about being present. I've got today. Maybe tomorrow. That'll have to be enough until the day after."

They stopped at the tideline. The incoming water washed over their feet, sending a shock of cool water up to Vivian's calves. "Colder than yesterday."

"Sun makes all the difference." Turning to face Vivian, Jackie said, "I'm not giving cancer the satisfaction of stealing what time I've got left. It can't have my mornings. Or my steps. Or take my sass."

"Couldn't if it wanted to," Vivian said.

"It's not about how many days I've got left, Viv. It's about how many I get to feel like me."

"In that case, let's give those terns a run for their money. One, two …"

"I want a video of that!"

Back in the kitchen, Mary Jo cradled a steaming mug of coffee, brewed from that overdesigned machine Vivian loved. Probably cost more than her first car.

She took a long sip, leaned against the counter, and smiled. The night before had been a riot. Those momma stories? Instant facelift for the soul. And bringing some levity to Jackie was the best medicine. Laughter as therapy. Laughter as anesthesia.

Her phone pinged.

She reached for it. *Here we go. Probably Sandy again, peddling another candle line or breakfast cruise. Nope. Fran's Family Photos.*

Fran Bass' granddaughter had taken over her photography and was hellbent on social engagement—group shots, candid outtakes, and the occasional *oopsie!* that went viral. One image was attached in Fran's text.

When Mary Jo tapped download, the caption loaded first: *$25 gift certificate for the best caption! Use it on your next head shot. Here's mine to start: Sugar Daddy or Granddaddy? Jury's still out. – Fran*

She waited while the image took its sweet time loading—spinning, buffering, making her stomach churn. Then ... *bam!*

"Oh, dear God."

Lori Anne, yawning, shuffled into the kitchen. "Mary Jo, that's takin' the Lord's name in—" Her phone dinged. She looked down. Froze. "OH. DEAR. LORD."

Down the hall, a door slammed open. Bertie called, "What's going on out here?"

Mary Jo didn't answer. She couldn't. Her eyes were locked on the screen, breath gone. Then another ping, loading a second picture. "Where's Viv?" she managed. "Where is she right now?"

"Beach," Bertie called. "Why? What's—"

Lori Anne held out her phone like it was contaminated.

Bertie stepped closer. Squinted. Froze. "Whooo," Bertie drawled, "is Arthur with?"

The woman beside him—young, pregnant, half-turned—wasn't clear. But his hand on her stomach said enough to Mary Jo.

"Viv cannot see this," Bertie snapped.

"That's what I'm saying," Mary Jo said. "Did she take her phone?"

"I'll check her room." Lori Anne ran out of the room.

"Who *is* that?" Bertie muttered again.

Mary Jo scanned the counter. "No phone here."

"She looks familiar." Bertie frowned. "But these days strangers look familiar to me."

From upstairs they heard, "Found it!"

Lori Anne came bounding back down the stairs holding a phone. "Is this it?"

Mary Jo snatched the phone and started pressing buttons. "They still on the beach?"

"On the boardwalk," Bertie answered. "Jackie's rinsin' her feet."

"We need to get the battery out," Mary Jo muttered, fumbling and turning the phone over. "How do you open—"

"Hurry. They're coming onto the porch," Bertie reported.

"This thing will go viral." Lori Anne tapped her own screen. "It's probably been screenshotted more times than a banana pudding recipe at a Baptist covered-dish."

Mary Jo was still clawing at the back of Vivian's phone. "Where is the battery cover? These new phones ... I don't think they even have a battery!"

"What if Jackie has her phone on her?" Lori Anne blew out a breath. "Should I check? How's Viv ever gonna recover from this?"

Mary Jo kept her gaze fixed on Vivian walking across the porch. "Or how will we?"

Chapter Fourteen

"Whew!" Vivian slid the glass door open and stepped inside. She kicked off her sandals, dropped her beach hat on the counter, and ran a hand through her windblown hair. "That walk wore me out. Jackie's energy is unreal! So ... have y'all eaten or should we whip up some brunch? Or coffee and muffins to hold us over? I'm game for anything today—shopping, a movie, maybe biking on the wildlife trail if this rain stops."

Silence.

She paused. Glanced around. "Don't all answer at once." She gave a short laugh, walked to the stairs. "I'm going to grab my phone."

Bertie leaned toward Lori Anne. "I'm not telling her."

"Well, don't look at me," Lori Anne muttered. "Mary Jo?"

Jackie stood near the porch door, staring down at her phone, unmoving. Her face had gone flat and pale. "Have y'all seen this?" She held out the screen, her voice low.

From upstairs, Vivian called, "Has anybody seen my phone?"

Lori Anne's voice dropped to a whisper. "I know. It's awful."

"Who is that hussy?" Jackie said.

"I'll distract her," Mary Jo said, already rising to her feet. Her stomach twisted. She didn't have a plan, just a need to get ahead of it. At the foot of the stairs, she turned and hissed, "You three better come up with something before I get back."

But Vivian's voice interrupted, closer now. "I swear I left it on the dresser. Did one of y'all pick it up by mistake? Bertie?"

Bertie blinked. "What are we talking about?"

"My phone."

"Oh. You have a phone? I should get one."

"Bertie, stop," Mary Jo said.

"Sorry. Thought she might, you know, fall for it."

"Fall for what?" Vivian's tone sharpened. Her eyes darted from one face to another. "What is going on with you four?"

No one answered.

Then Jackie stepped forward and extended her phone. "Here."

Vivian hesitated … then took the phone.

"Arthur," Jackie said.

Time slowed. Vivian tapped the screen, scrolled once. Froze.

Her heart thudded once, then stalled.

Her eyes locked on the image. Arthur's hand splayed across a woman's abdomen. His face downturned, smiling. The curve of the woman's stomach unmistakable. Her blouse lifted just enough to show the roundness.

The silence pressed in around her.

"Catch her," she heard Mary Jo whisper.

Vivian didn't fall. But something inside her did.

"That …" Her voice cracked. "No-good …"

She stared harder at the photo. Her breath caught. Her hands shook.

"Self-important …" Her volume climbed. "S.O.B. GYNECOLOGIST!"

She thrust the phone at Jackie, her jaw clenched, the rage clawing up her throat. "He's knocked up one of his patients!"

"Any idea who it is?" Mary Jo asked, barely above a whisper.

Vivian stared at the other image. "Can't make out her face. He's leaning over, blocking the view. Hand on her stomach like he owns it. But I'd bet my bottom dollar she won't live to see that baby born."

She lifted her gaze, dead cold.

"I'm gonna kill him. Then her."

Chapter Fifteen

"Viv." Jackie stepped toward her. "Come sit on the porch."

Vivian shook her head, eyes wide and burning. "No. The beach. I need the beach."

"Vivian, it's pouring and I—"

"STOP!" Vivian yanked the door open. "I'm sitting on the beach. Stay here if you want."

The other four didn't move. No one argued. Even the thunder held its breath.

The rain lashed sideways, but she didn't flinch. Gone was the polished hostess with her pearls and posture. Now the trip lay exposed—raw, stripped of charm and pretense—and the fury rising in her chest made her hands tremble.

One by one, she watched the others carry beach chairs through the rain not far from the tide line. Feet sinking into wet sand, clothes soaked through, they sat in silence, faces turned toward the gray-brown waves curling sideways.

"Lawd, help Viv," Bertie whispered.

"Yes, Lord," Lori Anne echoed. "Be with her now. Give her your strength to—"

"Don't you dare say it, Lori Anne. I don't want your Jesus strength to endure. I want the rage of the Devil."

"Viv, please," Mary Jo said. "Don't say stuff like that."

"I'm gonna do him like a dog that can't stop humping. Cut 'em off, both of 'em. Then his—"

Bertie reached over and clamped her hand over Vivian's mouth.

"That whore. She'll wish she'd never been born."

Bertie pulled her hand back. "Rain doesn't seem to be dampening the fire."

"Hell has no fury like ..." Lori Anne started.

"What do we do now?" Jackie asked. "This might be my last beach trip, and I don't want anything to steal the good times we have left."

Vivian looked down at the bracelet on her wrist—gold links intertwined with tiny diamonds. Every stone a milestone. The hand-engraved clasp, his promise. She clenched her jaw tight. "Asshole." She rose, unfastened the clasp, and held the bracelet in her palm. Her fingers closed around it, knuckles going white. "I'll tell you where I'm starting." She reached back to hurl it into the churning gray surf.

The splash barely registered over the wind.

Lori Anne bolted out of her chair. "Are you out of your ever-loving mind? Do you know how many syringes of Botox—I mean how many starving children that thing can feed?" Without waiting for a reply, she rushed toward the water and dove in headfirst, arms flailing, hair flying.

Jackie shot to her feet. "Are you crazy, Lori Anne? You can't swim!"

A few thrashes later, Lori Anne popped up, arm raised high. "Got it!" She stumbled to shore, mascara streaked to her chin, hair plastered flat. "Jesus walked on water." She gasped. "I dove in after diamonds. Miracles come in all forms, y'all."

"What do I care? I'm done with him."

"You're not thinking clear, Viv."

"Lori Anne's right," Mary Jo said. "Now's not the time to throw away ... I mean, Arthur, sure, but not the rest. Not us. Not everything you own."

"Play this right," Jackie said, "and you can take him to the cleaners. That summons last night—is it another wrongful death lawsuit against Arthur?"

"You got served with a summons?" Bertie asked.

"Last night, Bertie," Lori Anne said. "Keep up."

"Come on, Lori Anne," Mary Jo said.

"Sorry. I'm just pissed," Lori Anne replied.

"You cussed!" Jackie said.

"No I didn't," Lori Anne shot back.

"You said *pissed*."

"Piss is not a cuss word, Bertie. And I said I'm sorry."

"I'm cold," Vivian said. "And wet. And if anyone should be pissed, it's me. But right now, it's like God's the one who's—"

Bertie clamped her hand over Vivian's mouth again. "No need to say it. We get it."

Mary Jo stood. Gathering her chair, she said, "Who's up for a ride to the jewelry store?"

"Which one?" Jackie asked.

"She means where Arthur bought this fake love bracelet," Vivian said. "And, Mary Jo, that's about the best idea you've had since … well, ever."

Chapter Sixteen

Mary Jo whipped the Bronco into a tight parallel park on King Street—a small Charleston miracle, in Vivian's mind.

Vivian spotted the sign for Calhoun's and felt her chest tighten. Not from the heat hitting her as she opened the Bronco's front passenger door, but from what she'd come to leave behind. Without waiting for the others, she started up the sidewalk, her heels clacking on concrete. "Come on, y'all," she said over her shoulder, forcing her voice into something light. "My palm is itchin'. Momma said that means money's on the way—and I'm fixin' to get what's due me."

Mary Jo opened her door and leaned out. "I'll be along in a minute. I need to make a call."

"Bertie?" Vivian asked.

"Huh?"

"You coming?"

"Coming where?"

"Oh, for Pete's sake. Never mind."

Vivian reached for the heavy wooden door and pushed it open. The chime overhead didn't just ring. It resounded. Inside, the cool air smelled of gold polish and old wood, polished glass and the faint musk of estate jewelry that had outlived its owners. The scent of Charleston money and Charleston secrets—in Arthur's case, one he let slip too soon.

She led the way, her posture perfect, her pace deliberate. Every inch of her was composed—at least on the outside. Inside, her stomach turned. Not from nerves. From fury held so tight it had turned cold.

"Oh, if these walls could talk," Lori Anne said.

Let them talk. Let them whisper, Vivian thought. *Let them say she'd walked in a broken woman and left with her pride on the mend.*

Lori Anne reached out to stroke a velvet couch. Jackie scanned a jewelry case as if searching for a glazed donut filled with cream.

Vivian studied the young woman behind the counter. Then, her smile forming before she fingered the bracelet in her purse, she stepped forward. Her chin tilted enough to show lineage, not pride, as she took that first small step. "Hey there. Vivian Knox. My husband bought this for me a few weeks ago." She set the bracelet on the counter, her manicured nails clicking against the glass. The sound was clean. Final.

The saleswoman looked up and smiled. "Yes, ma'am. I remember. You came in last week and picked it up."

Vivian glanced at Lori Anne. A shrug—like *Well?*—was all the encouragement she needed. "I'd like to return it."

"You have the receipt?"

"Like you said, I came in and picked it up. There was no receipt. Already paid for."

"I'm sorry, ma'am but without a receipt …"

The fury came like a flood behind her eyes, but she kept the dam from breaking. Instead, she let her lips stretch out a touch further. Southern steel. "You got a boyfriend? Maybe the quarterback?"

"I'm sorry, what?"

"You're the head cheerleader, am I right?"

The girl's smile faltered.

"Been there. Stood where you're standing. I get it. Receipt. Received. Ownership. But here's the thing, suga. One day all that sparkle will fade. Friday nights end. Pom-poms go into the dumpster. You wake up one morning and realize you traded your twenties for touchdown dances and hollow promises of happily-ever-after."

Vivian heard Jackie whisper something, but she stayed on script.

"If you want, I can ring my manager."

"Oh, suga, there's no need for that. We're going to get along fine, you and me."

"I mean, if there is a problem with the quality …"

"No, that's not it. I loved it." She tapped the bracelet. "At first. But I changed my mind. Let's just say the sparkle wore off."

The clerk pulled out a small glass for inspection. "May I?"

"Please do."

The clerk bent over, inspecting the bracelet closely. "Seems fine."

"Always does until it's not, suga." Vivian tapped the diamond set. "Look right there. See how dull it is?"

She straightened. Her voice cautious, she said, "Mrs. Knox, I can assure you we inspected both bracelets and found nothing to suggest anything other than both were crafted with the utmost care and quality."

"And there it is." Turning to Jackie and Lori Anne, Vivian said loudly, "Hear that? *Both* bracelets." Vivian blinked, then let a sarcastic smile stretch a little wider. "How nice. How very, very nice."

Jackie whispered to the others, "Lord, help. Vivian learned that tone in charm school." Translation: she's about to blow.

"Care and quality? That's what I have right here. His utmost for his wife and …" Turning back to the clerk she asked, "Who'd you say the other one was for?"

"I, uh…" The clerk swallowed. "I'll need to speak with the store owner."

Vivian smiled. "Call her. Mrs. Manigault and me, we go way back. I'm sure she'll get this sorted out." Vivian pivoted and plopped down on a stool. "Go on, suga. I've got time to wait."

Back in the car, Mary Jo dialed, waited, then heard her call go to voicemail. "Baby, it's Mom. Call me as soon as you can. I think you know why." Pocketing her phone, she rested her head against the driver's window, a tear streaking her cheek, then the glass.

"MJ, you okay?"

"I will be. Someday."

"Is it about that thing you mentioned? The business with Charles' accountant?"

"Oh, that? No. I'm sure whatever that's about, it's not nearly as important as this."

Bertie's head appeared in Mary Jo's peripheral vision. "Come on, you tell me. You know I'll forget as soon as you do."

Mary Jo shifted in her seat. "You still have that picture on your phone?"

"I have a phone?"

"Stop messing with me. You know what I'm talking about. Pull it up. I want to see it again."

"Why not look on your phone?"

"I deleted it."

Bertie reached down for her pocketbook, swiped her phone, and handed it over the backrest for Mary Jo to see. "Sickening, isn't it?"

"You don't know the half of it." Reaching for the phone, Mary Jo asked, "May I?" She thumbed through Bertie's photos until she found the one she could erase from her phone but not her memory. "You have to admit, green is a good look on her."

The front passenger door opened.

"You better not let Viv hear you say that."

Vivian slid in, her smile small, cruel, and earned. "Hear what?"

Mary Jo handed the phone back to Bertie. "Well? Any luck?"

"A full refund. And Mrs. Manigault texted me a list of ten attorneys. She said the top three had billboards … and no mercy. By the time I'm finished with Arthur and his hussy, they'll wish they never laid eyes on each other."

"Did she happen to mention who the other woman was?" Mary Jo asked.

"No, but that's not important now. What is, right now, is spending more of Arthur's money. Girls, you up for it?"

"For what?" Bertie asked.

"A Charleston Harbor Boat cruise."

"Oh, that. God no. I get seasick," Jackie said.

"I hate tour boats," said Lori Anne.

"Not on this yacht you won't. You know that yacht what's his name lived on in *Fool's Gold*? The one with more square footage than my beach house? It rents for ten grand an hour."

"An hour?"

Vivian nodded. "And I think y'all can handle the harbor. Hell yeah! No way I'm gonna let Arthur think I'm sinking—not in Charleston Harbor. Not anywhere."

Chapter Seventeen

"Let's celebrate my freedom!" Vivian beamed, stepping from the Bronco.

"But, Viv, you don't even know if you're getting a divorce," Lori Anne replied.

"Oh, I know. And based on what Mrs. Manigault said, by the time the lawyers are finished with him, Arthur will be begging me to sign the divorce papers." She turned toward the marina office. "I'll go inside and see if that yacht's available."

"What? Don't tell me you're about to rent that expensive yacht!" exclaimed Jackie.

"Then there are bars on King Street and men galore." The passenger door on the Bronco slammed shut.

Mary Jo turned to the girls in the back and rested her elbow on the center console. "She's in that stage. The first one."

"Denial?" Lori Anne said. "Don't think so. She's blown through denial, anger, bargaining, and depression and gone straight to crazy."

"MJ, you have to tell her," Bertie said.

"Now's not the right time." *When will it ever be?* Mary Jo stared at the marina's front door, praying whatever craziness Vivian was up to wouldn't happen.

"Tell her what?" asked Jackie.

"Here she comes." Mary Jo pointed out the passenger window. "And she doesn't look happy."

"Mary Jo knows who the woman is wearing the green blouse," Bertie blurted out.

Jackie looked shocked. "You know the girl in the picture?" She grabbed her phone. "Oh dear God. Is that Virginia with Arthur? But how?"

"How do these things ever happen?" Bertie answered. "Arthur apparently has a zipper problem."

"I honestly thought he was being a father figure and looking after her since Charles died," Mary Jo said.

"Looking after her?" Lori Anne shot back. "Mary Jo, he was *after her*, period. This'll wreck Vivian."

"What the hell do you think it's doing to me?"

"Asshole," Bertie added.

The passenger door flew open. "Bad news, ladies. *Fool's Gold* is already out on a sail — next stop, lower King."

"MJ has something to tell you," Bertie blurted again.

Mary Jo shot Bertie a stare sharp enough to draw blood.

"Go on," Bertie continued. "Tell her."

Jackie's phone buzzed. "Hey, hon." She held up her hand for silence. "What's up?"

"What did I miss?" Vivian asked. "Don't tell me Sandy's photo-bombed us again."

"I've got so much to tell, but can we chat later?" Jackie mouthed, *It's Bill*. "Um, hum. Right. Oh, I remember, but ... yes."

"You have to tell her," Bertie repeated. "You promised." Mary Jo shot back, "Bertie, please stop!"

"Wait. What? Bill, you're not making any sense."

"Yes. And I will, but not now, not here while Jackie's on the phone."

Lori Anne said, "It's not about Sandy, Viv. It's a whole lot worse."

"Slow down, hon. I'm not following." The excitement in Jackie's voice drew all eyes back on her. "What? When?" Jackie's voice cracked. "You mean like right now?" She swiped at a tear.

"Of course, sure. I'll text you when I'm aboard. "Love you too." Hands trembling, Jackie slipped her phone into her purse.

"Suga, what is it?" Vivian asked.

"We have to get to the airport." Jackie dabbed both eyes. "Bill called in a favor from one of his Navy buddies. There's a military transport plane waiting for me at Joint Base Charleston."

"Now?" Vivian asked.

Mary Jo shifted into gear and backed out of the parking space. "*Thank you, Jesus!*"

"Has something happened?" Lori Anne asked. "Is Bill sick?"

Laughing through tears, Jackie shook her head. "Lord, no. He's meeting me in Zurich. There's a doctor who … Bill's got me in a group that's part of an experimental cancer treatment that's been having great results."

"Everyone, hold on." Mary Jo stomped the pedal and peeled out of the parking lot.

Vivian spun around in her seat. "Lori Anne, start prayin'. We've got Charleston traffic and forty-seven stoplights between us and the runway. We need divine intervention and a traffic angel with a lead foot."

Mary Jo honked twice and floored it. Lori Anne prayed out loud—calling down traveling mercies, open lanes, and protection from every crazy driver, including Mary Jo.

Out of the corner of her eye, Mary Jo caught Vivian glaring at her. "And you, missy. You better come clean and quick."

"Let's get to the airport first," Mary Jo answered. "Then we'll talk."

Chapter Eighteen

The rumble of airplanes, the airfield's sunbaked asphalt, and jet-fuel fumes served as Jackie's final goodbye. Mary Jo stood beside her Bronco, watching as the huge plane stood ready, green and hulking. Jackie climbed from the back seat and joined the group, her scarf whipping from a southwest wind, arms reaching.

The four other members of the SFG wrapped Jackie in a knot of hugs, all breath and heartbeat and holy silence.

Mary Jo cupped Jackie's cheeks, thumbs brushing fresh tears. "Go," she whispered. "Go get your miracle." She remained still as Jackie, with the assistance of two soldiers, ascended the stairs. Mary Jo's hands trembled at her sides. *Lord, let this work. Please let this work. She's hoped for too long to come up empty now. Please let this be the healing you promised.*

"Y'all, look at that," Vivian murmured. "Leopard flats, Vera Bradley tote ..."

At the top of the stairs, Jackie waved to the group.

"I swear," Vivian continued, "she's got that look—like the President boarding Air Force One."

Minutes later as the roar of the departing transport faded, its massive wings banking northward, Lori Anne said, "Hate to be a party pooper, but can you drop me at the Amtrak station?" Brushing away tears, she continued. "I've gotta get home."

"You're not coming with us?"

Lori Anne held up her phone. "Sammie texted during the drive. Emergency church meeting. Didn't want to say anything—Jackie's moment and all—but something's brewing."

"Sammie's not getting fired, is he?" Bertie asked.

"Oh, please. Sammie?" Lori Anne smirked. "He's fireproof. It's probably one of those church ladies overreacting to the new chandeliers in the sanctuary."

"What about your clothes?" asked Mary Jo.

"Sammie says we'll drive back down after this so-called emergency. As a pastor's wife, I can't fix every crisis with lipstick and laughter. But honey, I can stand by my man—with grace in my heart and stilettos on my feet."

Vivian pinched the bridge of her nose. "Wait. Let's take a breath. If you bail and Jackie's gone, that leaves—"

"Three," Bertie said. "And I know what you're thinking. How are we gonna lug their stuff out of the house?"

"I was going for that cuts our drinking party in half," Vivian deadpanned.

Mary Jo leaned close to Lori Anne. "You sure this isn't about something else?"

"Like Sammie cheating on me?" Lori Anne put both fists on her hips and struck a pose. "I work out to look like this and dress like this so other men will look. Sammie's the luckiest husband on the planet, and he knows it. He just said I needed to get home ASAP—that he needed me to corral the women in the church for some big announcement."

Vivian tried one last smile. "You sure I can't tempt you with a trip to King Charles' Place first? Celebrate me a bit?"

"Next train's in an hour. Gotta get a move on. There's always next year. And the year after."

Until there's not.

Outside the Amtrak station, Mary Jo hugged Lori Anne quick and tight. "Text when you know what's going on."

"And if it's about your pineapple casserole," Bertie said, "tell the deacons' wives to get over it."

The four of them laughed, then Lori Anne hurried through the doors and disappeared into the station.

Seated behind the wheel of the Bronco, Mary Jo took in the moment, a deep sadness washing over her. *And then there were three.*

"Now," Vivian said, climbing into the passenger seat. "Will you tell me what's worrying you?"

Mary Jo forced a laugh. "Who said I'm worried?"

"It's written all over your face, suga. Don't be concerned about me—Arthur's money cures all."

"Drinks first. Then we talk," Mary Jo answered. "Right, Bertie?"

"Um?"

"I said—"

"I know what you said." Bertie blinked. "Just ... not tracking what you mean."

Mary Jo gave her a quick wink. "Finally, we're on the same page."

They strolled into the hotel—high-end, over-scented, and swarming with tourists. Mary Jo passed a mirror in the lobby and barely recognized herself. Smudged mascara. Tight shoulders. A tiredness that ran marrow deep. "Piano bar?" she said. "Momma always said Cosmopolitans and music could fix anything."

Vivian smiled. "Gracious, this place is packed for so early in the afternoon. Bertie, scout us a table."

Mary Jo's phone buzzed. *Arthur.*

A second later, Vivian's screen lit up. "Oh, I can't believe this."

"Lori Anne?" Mary Jo asked. "She missed the train?"

"No, it's Arthur. Wants to talk. Probably realized I sold that bracelet and is worried I might buy a condo in Key West. Or it could be that he knows I've seen his disgusting photo." She shoved her phone into her purse. "Not replying. He's not worth the energy."

Mary Jo's phone buzzed again.

Arthur: Need to talk.

Vivian's phone rang—and kept ringing from inside her purse. Other patrons glanced over, as if annoyed.

Mary Jo watched her, heartbeat quickening. Then another ping on her phone.

Virginia: Mom, I got your voicemail. If you're with Vivian, get away from her. The store called about the bracelet. Arthur wants to come clean about us.

Mary Jo's breath caught. She looked up.

Vivian frowned down at her purse. "Oh, for the love of ..." She finally answered. "I'm not having this conversation with you right now, Arthur. I'm about to sit down with a Cosmopolitan or two. You'll have to wait."

Mary Jo leaned forward and hugged her. "I have to step out. But remember ... I love you, no matter what."

Bertie reappeared. "Found us a table by the front window. Ready?"

Vivian held up a hand, eyes still on Mary Jo. "Arthur asked if I'd talked to you yet about the baby-bump photo. What's he talking about?"

"You two grab the table," Mary Jo answered. "I need to call Virginia real quick. Won't take but a moment."

Vivian narrowed her eyes. "Fine. Bertie, hold our table. I'm going to the ladies' room. What I'm about to say shouldn't be heard in public."

Mary Jo walked briskly toward the entrance, her pulse pounding in her ears. *Just get through today. You can fall apart tomorrow.*

Outside, she turned and looked through the bar's front window. There, on the other side of the glass, sat Bertie. Alone. Scanning the lobby with a look of uncertainty. Her Cosmopolitan untouched, purse still on her lap, Bertie had the look of someone who'd forgotten why she was there.

Mary Jo's hand drifted to her chest.

It wasn't only Vivian she was afraid of losing.

It was time.

It was the SFG.

It was Virginia.

And in a moment of clarity, she knew what she had to do.

Her phone lit up again. She hesitated, then answered.

"Good Lord, Arthur. What in God's name have you done?"

Chapter Nineteen

"Oh, God, Mary Jo … you're the only one I can talk to."

"What the hell, Arthur?"

King Charles' Place rose beside her like a polished Southern matron—elegant and timeless with a hint of neglect evident in the chipped paint marking where maintenance and money clashed.

"Come on, Mary Jo, I need you."

"You mean I'm the only one taking your calls."

Mary Jo stood before the window, still watching Bertie inside and grateful there was no sign of Vivian. The mid-afternoon sun baked the historic brick facades, chasing tourists toward patches of shade provided by awnings. "We shouldn't be having this conversation. I can't even think right now, Arthur."

The rich, the opulent, those who wished to be noticed, drifted past in linen and seersucker, clutching shopping bags and iced lattes, their laughter bouncing off the glass storefronts of upscale boutiques and antique galleries.

"I need you more than ever, Mary Jo. You've always seen me—really seen me—and understood me better than anyone else."

Mary Jo turned away, embarrassed to be having this call in public. "But you've ruined everything—Vivian, my family, your family. What you've done to Virginia is disgusting."

"Remember the night I found out you were engaged to Charles?" His voice dropped an octave. "I drove to your apartment. I begged you not to marry him. I've loved you from the start, Mary Jo."

Her breath caught. "Why are you telling me this?"

"I thought ... I guess me saying it would help you understand how much I've always loved you, even all those years ago."

"What was I supposed to do? Give Charles back his ring? Burn my friendship with Vivian to the ground?"

Somewhere above on a rooftop bar, the thump of bass and clink of cocktail glasses hinted at happy hour.

"After your first date, Viv was already doing cartwheels down the hall, claiming you were her forever love. She adored how you lit up a room. How you made her feel. And now, she'll be a wreck for who knows how long."

"Have you ever thought"—Arthur hesitated—"what could've been ... with us?"

"Are you drunk? Because if you're sober and hitting on me after you got my daughter pregnant and broke my best friend's heart—"

"You have, haven't you? Thought about us."

"Well, of course, Arthur. Every time Viv tells me how you've pulled another stunt, I thank God I married Charles and not you."

"Now you're just being mean."

"I'm hanging up. I need to call Virginia and warn her about what a stupid jackass you are."

"Why do you think you were always at our home for almost every occasion after Charles died? I just wanted to be near you. What happened to us?"

"What happened to *us*? There was NEVER an us!"

Vivian reappeared at the table. Mary Jo, wanting to keep an eye on Bertie but not wishing to be seen eased closer to the curb to put a threesome of women between her and the window. "Don't call me again, Arthur."

"Mary Jo, listen. When I drove all the way to Rock Hill that night thinking—hoping—you wanted me the way I wanted you

... When we kissed, when we ... God, Mary Jo, I thought that meant—"

"Please stop this nonsense!"

"Haven't you ever let someone get away, had regrets, and wondered how it might have been?"

From above the heads of one of the women, Mary Jo saw Bertie pointing at the window. Wheeling around, she started up the sidewalk, dodging tourists.

"I'm serious," he insisted. "Don't tell me there wasn't a spark between us."

"Why are you talking about *US*?" Her jaw tightened. Her voice came low. "My mother saw right through you. I'm hanging up now."

"No, wait, Mary Jo! There's one more thing you need to know."

"I have to go. Your wife is about to wring my neck for not telling her sooner—like I had a heads-up. Goodbye, Arthur."

"It's Virginia."

"What about Virginia?"

"She reminds me of you. Her long brown hair, those emerald-green eyes. When I'm with her, I'm with you."

Mary Jo snapped, "You are SICK! Damn, Arthur! She's my daughter! Our families traveled together. Our girls are like sisters."

"I know. And now you and I can raise my son and your grandson together. Or daughter. I'm good with either. You know how it is with the first one. The mother needs her mother close.

"If I have anything to do with it, you and Virginia will never see each other again. And I can promise that you and I will never be in the same room together. Don't call me again. I'm blocking this number."

Vivian grabbed her arm. "Mary Jo!"

Thrusting her phone at Vivian, Mary Jo said, "Talk some sense into your husband. I'm done trying." Shaking free of Vivian's grasp, she bolted across the street, narrowly missing a horse and carriage.

From behind her, Vivian yelled, "Wait! We have to talk!"

But it was too late. Mary Jo escaped into a boutique and then quickly back out through a side door. Checking the alley, she walked west, away from the carnage behind her.

Chapter Twenty

The alley cloaked Mary Jo in shadows, narrow and uninviting. Rusted downspouts clung to the brick walls, weeping from the afternoon shower she'd driven through after dropping off Lori Anne at the Amtrak station. Somewhere on a rooftop above, a pigeon cooed with unsettling cheer. She moved slowly—sneakers scuffing against uneven cobblestone.

The air reeked of fryer oil and old citrus—maybe lemons once crushed for cocktails and dumped without ceremony from the restaurant on her right. She pressed one hand to the wall, steadying herself, the cool brick biting into her palm. A breeze stirred something rank from a nearby trash bin, bringing with it black flies. She stood frozen, the sun pinning her shadow to the alley and its protection.

She had run. Not from danger. From them—Vivian, Arthur, Virginia, the truth. She hated the thought of Bertie still sitting alone at the table, waiting. But she had to get away just to clear her head. Poor Bertie. Would she give up? Get up? Walk out and wander off?

Mary Jo's stomach turned.

She hadn't cried. She could now. The rush of it all overwhelmed her. But the strangest part was she didn't want to give in. Not yet. Not until she was back in her Bronco and heading to the beach house to get her things. She'd clear out before Viv and Bertie could catch a ride back and that would be that. The end of it all. The end of the SFG.

Thanks, Arthur. Thanks for destroying everything I love, all that I had left.

The world tilted slightly off its axis. It wouldn't crash. Life wouldn't break. No, it would simply and slowly slide away until there was nothing left to gather except broken pieces.

God, how on earth would she ever help Virginia navigate this mess?

It's times like this, when I miss Charles the most. He'd know what to say, what to do, be there to hold her while she sobbed.

I hate you, Arthur. You've ruined everything.

A horse clip-clopped past the mouth of the alley, the carriage driver calling out facts about Charleston's haunted mansions and "the oldest garden in the city." Tourists filmed with their phones. Mary Jo turned away. With her gaze fixed on the eave where the pigeon cooed, she stared at the blue slice of sky between buildings and wondered how anything could still be so bright.

"Mary Jo?"

His voice. Steady. Familiar. A little raspy from the years. But also softer.

She turned and looked up the alley. Ted? He stood in The Indigo Room's back doorway.

"I … I wasn't sure," he stammered. Your hair … it's …" Stunned, she reached for the only weapon that remained— wit. "Turning grayer by the second."

"I was going to say the same style I remember. My God, I can't believe it's really you." He took a moment to look past her, then back up the alley toward King Street. "What're you doing out here?"

Her knees nearly gave way. The tears came rushing up. "I— it's a long—" she choked out.

"Hey," he said gently, stepping close and catching her as she buckled forward into his arms. "Hey. I've got you."

And she broke. A great dam of pain bursting. A trickle at first, then a torrent. Not loud, but fully—with the shuddering kind of shattering that happens from the inside out, where breath hitching becomes sobbing, and sobbing becomes something wordless and wild. Her fists curled against his chest, clutching the soft cotton of his shirt as if she needed it to breathe.

He didn't flinch. Didn't speak. Just held her close and rocked her gently, like a man who'd once lost something too—and had found it again. His breath warmed the crown of her head, its slow, patient rhythm keeping pace with her unraveling.

Her body betrayed her. The longing for touch—to be seen, cradled, and kept safe—allowed her to collapse into him. Pressing her cheek into his shirt, she took in the scent of his aftershave. She let go of all the chains that bound her. Her memory of Charles, her love for Virginia, her hatred for Arthur, her eternal bond with Vivian, and the fractured family of the SFG.

And into that space—against his chest, warm, damp, in heaving sobs—came something she didn't expect. The pulse of being a woman. Not a mother. Not a friend. Not the keeper of secrets or the fixer of messes. But a woman held. Desired. Needed.

Her breathing slowed. Her ribs ached. And something moved inside her—a pressing presence too firm to be ignored.

When the roughness of his chin scraped against her forehead, sliding down and then along the top of her cheek, she gave in. With eyes closed, she tilted her mouth upward to meet his. Tears seeped into the edges of her mouth. "I'm so sorry," she whispered. "I—this isn't how I wanted to see you again."

His lips found hers, and no more words were necessary.

They clutched each other amidst the alley smells—two people carrying years, pain, and pieces of something that once had been first love.

And maybe—just maybe—still was.

Chapter Twenty-One

On a very fine day in October, Mary Jo brought her Bronco around to the door of the Columbia Regional Hospital. Vivian opened the passenger door and watched Lori Anne wheel Virginia out the front doors and to the curb. Virginia rose from the wheelchair and, with Vivian's help, eased herself and her newborn into the back seat. The sunlight poured through the back windshield—warm and full—with the kind of brilliance you don't notice until you've been without it awhile.

The odor of the hospital lobby still clung to Vivian's blouse—antiseptic and sterile—but in the breeze, the freshness of cut grass marked a new chapter for all. Fall would come, then winter, but the promise of spring and new life offered hope. Love and faith—and always hope.

Virginia—pale, radiant, but still weak—tucked a blanket gently around baby Caroline's legs.

"You good back there?" Mary Jo asked softly.

Vivian reached across Virginia and pulled the seatbelt across mother and child. "Drive slowly and we'll be fine."

"Always."

"No, not always. There was that time on I-95 when you raced along the shoulder at close to ninety to get past that line of cars."

"That was different," Mary Jo answered. "You were in labor with Georgia."

Still bent over, Vivian fiddled with the buckle, and Caroline's tiny hand clutched a lock of Vivian's hair.

"My gosh, Virginia, she looks just like you at that age."

Mary Jo asked from the driver's seat, "Not Arthur?"

Silence.

"Too soon?" Mary Jo added.

"Never is too soon."

Jackie leaned over Vivian's shoulder for another look. "I think I'll ride with Virginia in the back seat. Is that okay?"

"You can be on spit-up patrol," Vivian answered.

"Bertie and I will follow behind you," Lori Anne said, lifting her sunglasses to dab her eyes. "No rush."

Vivian slipped into the front passenger seat and adjusted the strap on her purse. She'd lost weight at True North Wellness Center along with another kind of weight. The sort that doesn't show on scales but settles in your heart.

"So, update me. Jackie, you're glowing," said Vivian. "I mean that. Your color's better."

The Bronco pulled away, creeping at such a low speed that Vivian murmured under her breath, "We may not reach the entrance before Christmas."

Mary Jo shot her a glance. "You said slow."

"The tumors shrank," Jackie answered. "Not gone but smaller. And my doctor says they may eventually go away completely."

"But your hair?" Vivian replied. "It's so curly and—"

"White? You can say it."

"Silver," Mary Jo said. "Regal and radiant."

"How about you, Viv?" Jackie asked. "We haven't talked about … *it*. And you don't have to now if you don't want to."

Vivian felt strength in the warmth of the sun, in the comfort of once more being among friends who knew all her secrets and didn't judge. "Every day's a gift. It's up to me to make of it what I will. But this is Virginia's moment." With a wink directed at Mary Jo, Vivian smiled the kind of smile that didn't need explanation. "Sometimes you simply have to step off the stage."

"Even when you've tried to be the focus your whole life, right?" asked Mary Jo.

"Something like that," said Vivian. "At rehab, they helped me take responsibility, make amends, admit the lies, and accept help. It's all related to total wellness steps stages. I'm just not ready to talk about it now."

"But the lawsuit?" Jackie asked. "Did they depose you?"

"Ongoing. And my lawyer said it helps that Arthur and I are both in counseling and I went through rehab. He says that as long as we're married, I won't be forced to testify about the other lawsuits against Arthur, and I'm okay with that. I played a part in the mess too. I've been in denial for so long I forgot how strong I could be when it's needed."

Jackie reached over the seat and squeezed Vivian's shoulder. "I'm proud of you."

Vivian couldn't answer. Just looked away, watching the hospital parking deck fade from view.

"Jackie, did you talk to Lori Anne?" Mary Jo asked.

"About?"

"Their forced church plant."

"That's a euphemism for church split," Vivian offered. "Lori Anne can give you the details. She did say that the two of them now co-teach, co-preach on Sundays. She reads the Scripture; Sammie preaches. The congregation is encouraged to text questions, and Lori Anne pitches them to Sammie. She's not exactly teaching and preaching. More like facilitating with glitter eye shadow and tight jeans … Preacher's Wife 2.0."

"But if I know Lori Anne," Mary Jo said, "she'll have a comment or two to add."

"Exactly," Vivian echoed.

Virginia remained quiet, her gaze fixed on the side mirror. Vivian caught Bertie waving from Lori Anne's Lexus. And there it was—something wild and warm and impossibly young erupted inside. An old thrill. A memory of the five of them barreling down highways toward Myrtle Beach or Fort Lauderdale, eager to grab all of life they could juggle.

A different road trip, yes. Shorter, to be sure. And they weren't chasing parties or sunburns or boys, but something equally gratifying: grandparenthood. Imperfect, unplanned, and not the way she'd expected to spend her golden years, but the thrill of what was to come stirred her.

Mary Jo would be a grandmother, yes, and Ted a fun grandpa—if the two of them could ever settle on a wedding date.

But so would she, in her own strange, stitched-together way. She, baby Caroline's godmother … to Arthur's child. The bond of friendship, the love of roommates, had a way of redeeming the crooked lines, of turning even the shattered into something whole again. And for the first time in a long while, Vivian felt ready—not only to forgive, but to live her part in what came next.

The road ahead was winding, unknown, and yet, somehow, the five of them would be fine.

They always were.

Next Chapter

In the end, the Second Floor Girls didn't ride off into the sunset. They walked arm in arm into Virginia's apartment—a little wrinkled, a little wiser, carrying stories they would only tell baby Caroline.

Jackie boarded a plane to chase hope, giving the SFG permission to believe again. Always the brave one, she left them, courage tucked beneath unseen wings.

Vivian released the weight of a reputation she could never escape.

Lori Anne kept them laughing, praying, and slightly off balance the way she always had—with humor laced in hard truth.

Bertie became proof that love outlives memory, a reminder that even when disease takes someone from your life, it never takes them from your story.

And Mary Jo? She rediscovered her voice—and the man who once made her heart race.

Life had cracked them open, but it never broke them.

Years from now, when the road stretched out before them, they'd still remember Highway 501—the rusted Dino sign at the old convenience store, the Camaro packed with girls, the blue lights flashing, and Bertie's fearless grin as she said, "You buyin'?" They'd remember how young they were, how invincible they felt. And they'd remember this too—how time had humbled them, healed them, and bound them tighter than ever.

Between heartbreak and healing, between sunburns and sacred prayers, they always had something better than perfect.

Each other.

Scan the QR code to enjoy Jane's award-winning books or to book Jane for your next event.

Scan the QR code to listen to Jane's live presentation.

www.ingramcontent.com/pod-product-compliance
Lightning Source LLC
LaVergne TN
LVHW040105080526
838202LV00045B/3777